ABOUT THE AUTHORS

KEVIN J. ANDERSON and his wife, **REBECCA MOESTA,** have been involved in many STAR WARS projects. Together, they are writing the eleven volumes of the YOUNG JEDI KNIGHTS saga for young adults, as well as creating the JUNIOR JEDI KNIGHTS series for younger readers. Rebecca Moesta is also writing the second trilogy of JUNIOR JEDI KNIGHTS adventures.

Kevin J. Anderson is the author of the STAR WARS: JEDI ACADEMY trilogy, the novel *Darksaber*, and the comic series THE SITH WAR and THE GOLDEN AGE OF THE SITH for Dark Horse comics. He has written many other novels, including two based on *The X-Files* television show. He has edited three STAR WARS anthologies: *Tales from the Mos Eisley Cantina,* in which Rebecca Moesta has a story; *Tales from Jabba's Palace*; and the forthcoming *Tales of the Bounty Hunters*.

STAR WARS

YOUNG JEDI KNIGHTS

JEDI UNDER SIEGE

KEVIN J. ANDERSON
and REBECCA MOESTA

BERKLEY JAM BOOKS, NEW YORK

STAR WARS: YOUNG JEDI KNIGHTS
JEDI UNDER SEIGE

A Berkley Jam Book / published by arrangement with
Lucasfilm Ltd.

PRINTING HISTORY
Boulevard edition / September 1996
Berkley Jam edition / April 1998

The Penguin Putnam Inc. World Wide Web site address is
http://www.penguinputnam.com

Check out the Ace Science Fiction/Fantasy newsletter,
and much more, at Club PPI!

ISBN: 0-425-16633-3

BERKLEY JAM BOOKS®
Berkley Jam Books are published by The Berkley Publishing Group,
a member of Penguin Putnam Inc.,
200 Madison Avenue, New York, New York 10016.
BERKLEY JAM and its logo are are trademarks
belonging to Berkley Publishing Corporation.

PRINTED IN THE UNITED STATES OF AMERICA

To Letha L. Burchard
a supporter, fan, and friend
who "knew us when" . . .

and is still speaking to us

acknowledgments

The usual round of thanks to Lillie E. Mitchell, whose flying fingers transcribe our dictation and whose dedication to our characters and stories keeps our interest focused; Lucy Wilson, Sue Rostoni, and Allan Kausch at Lucasfilm for their above-and-beyond-the-call helpful suggestions and open minds; Ginjer Buchanan and the folks at Berkley/Boulevard for their wholehearted support and encouragement over the course of this entire series; and Jonathan MacGregor Cowan for being our most avid test reader and brainstormer.

JEDI UNDER SIEGE

1

IN THE UNCERTAIN predawn light, Jaina watched her uncle, Luke Skywalker, maneuver the *Shadow Chaser* into the Jedi academy's hangar bay at the base of the Great Temple. Her father, Han Solo, and Chewbacca had not even stayed long enough to perform that chore after the young Jedi Knights returned from the Wookiee homeworld of Kashyyyk.

With the Shadow Academy on the move, they had no time to lose.

Jaina found it hard to believe that barely two days earlier Kashyyyk had been under attack by Imperial forces led by none other than her friend Zekk, now a Dark Jedi in the service of the Second Imperium. When she'd confronted the dark-haired young man in the forest underlevels, he had warned her not to return to Yavin 4 because the Shadow Academy would soon attack.

Jaina had to believe the warning was a

sign that Zekk still cared about her and her twin brother Jacen.

She and her friends had been back on Yavin 4 for only a few minutes. None of them had gotten much sleep on the swift hyperspace flight back, but they all ran on adrenaline. Jaina felt as if she would explode if she couldn't *do* something right away. So many preparations to make, so much to plan.

Standing beside her near the entrance to the hangar bay, Jacen gave her a nudge. When she glanced at him, his brandy-brown eyes looked straight into hers. "Hey, it'll be *okay*," he said. "Uncle Luke will know what to do. He's been through plenty of Imperial attacks."

"Sure, that makes me feel a lot better," she answered, not believing it for a minute.

As usual, Jacen resorted to one of his favorite weapons to get her mind off the battle that was sure to come. "Hey, want to hear a joke?"

"Yes, Jacen," said Tenel Ka, striding up to join them. "I believe humor could be of some use now." The warrior girl from Dathomir glistened with perspiration from having spent the last ten minutes running "to stretch her muscles" in an effort to work off her own tension.

"Okay, Jacen. Fire away," Jaina said, pretending to brace herself for the worst.

Tenel Ka pushed back her long, reddish-gold braids with one arm. Her left arm had been severed in a terrible accident during lightsaber training, and she refused to accept a synthetic replacement. She nodded to Jacen. "You may proceed with the joke."

"Okay, what time is it when an Imperial walker steps on your wrist chronometer?" Jacen raised his eyebrows, waiting. "Time to get a new chronometer!"

After a heartbeat of dead silence, Tenel Ka nodded and said in a serious voice, "Thank you, Jacen. Your humor was quite . . . adequate."

The warrior girl never cracked a smile, but Jaina thought she detected a twinkle in her friend's cool gray eyes. Jaina was still groaning in mock agony when Luke and the young Wookiee Lowbacca climbed out of the *Shadow Chaser*.

Deciding there wasn't a moment to lose, Jaina hurried over to them. Apparently Uncle Luke must have felt the same way—when Jacen and Tenel Ka trotted up behind Jaina, the Jedi Master began to speak without pre-amble.

"It'll take the Second Imperium some time to install the new computer components they stole for their fleet," Luke said. "We may have a few days yet, but I don't want to take any chances. Lowie—Tionne and Raynar went out to the temple on the lake for a training exercise. I'd like you to take your T-23 and go bring them back here. We all need to work together."

Lowie roared an acknowledgment and sprinted for the small skyhopper his uncle Chewbacca had given him. From the clip at Lowie's waist the miniaturized translating droid Em Teedee said, "Why certainly, sir. It would be Master Lowbacca's great pleasure to be of service. Consider it done." Reprimanding the little droid for its embellishments with an absent growl, the young Wookiee climbed into the small T-23 and closed the canopy.

Luke turned to the warrior girl from Dathomir. "Tenel Ka, gather as many students as you can and give them a crash course in ground combat against terrorist attacks. I'm not sure what strategies the Shadow Academy will use, but I can't think of anyone better to teach them about commando tactics than you."

"Yeah, she was great against those Bartokk assassins on Hapes," Jacen said.

Tenel Ka surprised Jaina by blushing pink before she gave a curt nod and sped off on her assignment.

"What about Jacen and me, Uncle Luke?" Jaina asked, bursting with impatience. "What should we do? We want to help."

"Now that the *Millennium Falcon* is gone, we need to get the new shield generators back up and running to protect us from an aerial attack. Come with me."

The primary equipment for the Jedi academy's new defensive shield generators was located in the jungle across the river, but the shields were controlled from the Comm Center. Han Solo had recently brought the components from Coruscant as a stopgap measure while the New Republic scrambled to assemble a major defense against the impending Imperial attack.

"Hey, should I send a message to Mom?" Jacen asked, sitting down at one of the consoles.

"Not until we know more," Luke answered.

"Your dad and Chewie were going to contact her and explain everything once they were under way. Leia has her hands full mustering troops to station here as permanent protectors for the Jedi academy. At the moment, *we've* got to do everything we can to guard it ourselves.

"Meanwhile, Jacen, monitor all the communications bands. See if you can pick up any signals, especially ones that might be Imperial codes. Jaina, let's get those shield generators powered up and running."

"Already on it, Uncle Luke." Jaina grinned at him from the control station. "Shields are up and at full strength. Guess I should run a complete readiness check, though, just to make sure there are no gaps in our defenses."

Jacen put on a headset and began scanning through the various comm frequencies. No sooner had he begun than a loud crackle erupted from the earpiece, followed by a familiar voice.

". . . requesting permission for landing and all that usual stuff. Here I come. *Lightning Rod* out."

"Hey, wait!" Jacen said into the voice pickup, on the verge of panic. "You can't do that—I mean, we have to drop our shields first. Give me a minute, Peckhum."

"Shields? What shields?" the old spacer's voice came back. "Me and the *Lightning Rod* been doin' the supply run to Yavin 4 for years now. Never had to worry about shields before."

"We'll meet you down at the landing pad and explain everything," Jacen said. "Hang on a minute."

"Am I going to need a code to get in?" Peckhum asked. "No one gave me any codes before I left Coruscant. Nobody told me about any shields."

Jacen looked up at Luke. "It's old Peckhum in the *Lightning Rod*," he said. "Does he need a code to get in?"

Luke shook his head and motioned for Jaina to drop the shields. Jaina bent over the control console, her lower lip caught between her teeth. After a minute she said, "There, that ought to do it. Shields lowered again."

For some reason, now that the shields were down Jacen felt a cold tingle of vulnerability run up the back of his neck. "Okay, Peckhum," he said, "you're clear to land. But make it quick, so we can power up again."

• • •

When the old spacer stepped out of his battered supply shuttle, he looked the same as every other time Jacen had seen him: pale skin, long lanky hair, grizzled cheeks, and rumpled flight suit.

"Come on, Peckhum," Jacen said. "I'll help you get the supplies inside. We need to hurry, before the Imperials get here."

"Imperials?" The spacer scratched his head. "Is that why you've got energy shields up? Are we under attack?"

"It's okay," Jacen said, impatient to get the *Lightning Rod* unloaded. "The shields are back up. You just can't see them."

The old spacer craned his neck to stare up into the misty white sky of the jungle moon. "And the attack?"

"Well, we heard a rumor—a pretty solid one." He hesitated. "From Zekk. He's the one who led the raid on the computer fabrication facility on Kashyyyk—and he warned Jaina that the Shadow Academy is on its way. We'd better get inside."

Old Peckhum looked at Jacen in alarm. The teenager Zekk had been like a son to him; they had lived together in the lower city levels on Coruscant . . . until Zekk had been kidnapped by the Shadow Academy.

As a familiar cold tingle crept up the back of Jacen's neck, Peckhum whispered, "Too late." He pointed into the sky. "They're already here."

2

FROM THE HIGHEST observation turret on the Shadow Academy, Brakiss—Master of all the new Dark Jedi—looked down at the insignificant green speck of the jungle moon. The devastating assault was about to begin, and before long Yavin 4 and its Jedi academy would be crushed under the might of the Second Imperium.

As it should be.

Through the winding metal corridors of the station, stormtroopers manned their battle stations, newly trained TIE pilots conducted preflight checks on their ships, and the eager Dark Jedi students prepared for their first major victory.

The ultimate battle would be a two-pronged assault led jointly by the most powerful of the new Nightsisters, Tamith Kai, and Brakiss's own protégé, dark-haired Zekk, whose enthusiasm to make something significant of his life had left him an easy target for conversion to the dark side.

Brakiss closed his eyes and drew a deep breath of the recycled air that rushed through the ventilation shafts. His silvery robes swirled around him.

Though he stood isolated here, he could sense the accelerating preparations affecting everyone in the spiked station; tensions mounted, as did hunger for battle. In the undercurrent of swirling thoughts, he clearly felt the troops' dedication to the Second Imperium's great leader, Emperor Palpatine. He also detected an undertone of anxiety over the coming attack, but this only made his lips curl upward. Fear would give an added edge to their fighting abilities, enough to make them cautious . . . but not enough to paralyze them.

Brakiss longed to see Luke Skywalker defeated. Years ago, he had infiltrated the Jedi academy as a student to absorb the methods the New Republic taught, then bring them back to the remnants of the Empire. But Brakiss hadn't been able to fool the Jedi Master. Instead, Skywalker had tried to turn him away from his devotion, undermine his dedication to the Second Imperium. Skywalker had tried to "save" him—he thought with a sneer—and Brakiss had fled.

But because of his willingness to dabble in the dark side, Brakiss had by then learned enough to form his own Dark Jedi training center.

Now it would be a marvelous showdown.

Beside him, the air shimmered. Brakiss opened his calm, beatific eyes and sensed an ominous static surrounding the projection of the Emperor. The mysterious great leader of the Second Imperium hovered in front of him in holographic form, a cowled head as tall as Brakiss's entire body, a towering image with glittering yellow eyes and a wrinkled face pinched by shadows.

"I grow eager for my domination again, Brakiss," the Emperor said.

"And I am eager to give it to you, my master," Brakiss answered, bowing his head.

Accompanied by four of his powerful red Imperial guards, the Emperor himself had recently taken up residence on the Shadow Academy, arriving in a special armored shuttle. While the fearsome, scarlet-clad guards kept all prying eyes away, the Emperor remained sealed in an opaque isolation chamber. Palpatine had never spoken directly to his loyal Shadow Academy subjects, nor had he even conversed face-to-face with Brakiss. The Emperor had appeared only in holographic transmissions.

"We are ready to launch our strike, my Emperor," Brakiss said. He glanced up at the forbidding image. "My Dark Jedi guarantee you victory."

"Good—because I have no wish to wait further," the Emperor's image said. "The remainder of my newly constructed fleet has not yet arrived, though they shall be here within hours. My Imperial warships are presently being refitted with the computer systems stolen from Kashyyyk. My guards report that many vessels are ready to fight, and the rest will be finished shortly."

Brakiss bowed again, clasping his hands in front of him. "I understand, my lord. But let us withhold the military strike force for our next major assault on the more heavily guarded worlds of the Rebel Alliance. On Yavin 4, we have only a few weakling do-gooder Jedi to deal with. They should cause no problem for my Force-trained soldiers."

Inside his shadowy cowl, the Emperor looked skeptical. "Do not let your overconfidence betray you."

Brakiss continued speaking with greater passion. He let his feelings come to the fore, hoping to convince his great leader. "With this important strike on the Jedi academy, the Second Imperium becomes more than just an undisciplined band of pirates raiding equipment. We mean to retake the *galaxy*, my lord. This battle must be a battle of philosophies, of willpower. This is the *Imperial* way against the *Rebel* way—and so it should be my trainees against Skywalker's, Jedi versus Jedi. A shadow play, if you will, of darkness against light. We still intend to harass them with TIE fighter strikes from the air, but the main conflict will be direct and personal—as it must be! We can crush their very hearts, not merely breach their defenses."

Brakiss smiled, looking up to meet the glowing yellow eyes of the Emperor. "And when we defeat them utterly with the powers of the dark side, the remainder of the Rebels will scatter and hide, trembling at their own nightmares, as we recapture what is rightfully ours."

The Emperor's holographic face did something frighteningly unusual. The withered, puckered lips curled in a satisfied *smile*.

"Very well. It shall be as you request, Brakiss—Jedi against Jedi. You may begin your assault when ready."

3

THE SHADOW ACADEMY dropped its
cloaking device, dissolving its shield of invis-
ibility. As the spiked station appeared over
Yavin 4, two specially equipped TIE fighters
dropped out of its launching bay. Silently
moving in tandem, they plunged into the
misty atmosphere.

The fighters had been coated with a stealth
hull plating to blur their sensor signatures,
and the output from their high-powered
twin ion engines had been damped. Their
mission was to strike in secret, not to provide a show of force.

Commander Orvak swooped into the lead,
while the second TIE fighter, flown by his
subordinate Dareb, flanked him. Together,
they shot around the small moon and skimmed lower into the atmosphere, spiraling
entirely around the equator back to the coordinates of the ancient temple ruins where
Skywalker had established his Jedi academy.

Orvak flew with the controls gripped in his black-gloved hands. He felt the quiet thrumming of the Imperial fighter's engines as if he were riding an untamed beast of burden. He piloted with careful concentration, dancing on the air currents, buffeted by thermal updrafts from the jungle below.

"Keep steady," he muttered to himself. This commando run would require the utmost precision and piloting skill. Along with a new batch of TIE fighter trainees chosen from the ranks of young stormtroopers, Orvak had completed the simulations over and over again en route to the Yavin system.

But this was the real thing. Now the Emperor was depending on him.

Massassi trees formed a chaotic carpet of green below. Gnarled branches thrust above the thick canopy like monster claws. Orvak glided in low, watching the wake of his passage disturb treetop creatures who fled from the blast of his hot exhaust.

His companion Dareb spoke over a tight line-of-sight beamed channel. The other pilot's words were encrypted and descrambled by a special coding system in Orvak's cockpit. "Long-range sensors are picking up the protective energy field," Dareb said. "The shield generators are right where our covert information said they would be."

"Target verified," Orvak acknowledged, speaking into the microphone built into his helmet. "Lord Brakiss, who endured some time here, knows much of the layout of the Jedi academy itself—if the Rebels haven't moved things around."

"Why would they?" Dareb said. "They're far too complacent, and we are about to show them their folly."

"Just don't show me *your* folly," Orvak said. "Enough chatter. Head for the target."

The invisible shields hovered like a protective umbrella over a section of jungle where a river sliced through the trees and an ancient-looking stone pyramid rose majestically. Orvak hoped that by the end of this day Skywalker's Great Temple would no longer be standing.

But before the Shadow Academy could begin the primary assault, Orvak and Dareb had to complete their preliminary mission: to knock out that shield generator and open the doors wide for a devastating attack.

Orvak checked his sensors. In the infrared and other portions of the electromagnetic spectrum, he could see the deadly ripples of the hovering force field dome that protected the Jedi academy. Yet, because of the tall Massassi trees, the shield did not reach all the way to the ground, halting instead five meters above the treetops. Five meters—a shallow gap between foliage and sizzling energy, but wide enough for a crack pilot to negotiate. Here and there, a few upthrust branches were singed and blackened where they had intruded into the crackling energy dome.

"It'll be a tight squeeze," Orvak said. "Ready for it?"

"I feel like I could take on the whole Rebel Alliance by myself," Dareb said.

Orvak didn't acknowledge this display of overconfidence. "Closing in," he said.

He brought the stealth TIE fighter lower, just skimming the treetops. Leaves whispered beneath him, chattering and scratching against the wings of his ship. The air seemed to ripple in front of the fighter, a faint indication of the energy shield, and he hoped the sensors were correct.

"Stay on target," he said. "Once we get under the shields, our real work starts."

Just as they passed underneath the invisible boundary, Dareb swerved to one side to avoid an unexpected moss-covered branch that elbowed up only a meter above the canopy. The young pilot overcompensated and struck a corner of his square wing panel against another branch, which sent him tumbling.

"I can't hold it!" he shouted into the comm system. "I'm out of control!"

Dareb's TIE fighter pinwheeled up into the deadly force field and exploded as it hit the disintegrating wall. Intent on his mission, Orvak streaked onward, looking into the rear viewers to see the flaming debris of his partner tumbling out of the sky.

He clenched his teeth and drew a deep breath through the oxygen mask in his helmet. "We're all expendable," Orvak said, as if trying to convince himself. "Expendable. The mission is all-important. Dareb was my backup. So now it's up to me. Alone." He swallowed hard, knowing that now the Rebels must be aware of his covert mission.

Without pause, Orvak homed in on the isolated shield-generating station. The machinery looked like a set of tall disks half buried in the jungle underbrush, surrounded by a cleared maintenance area that provided just enough space for him to land his small Imperial fighter. Visible in the distance rose the great pyramid that housed Skywalker's Jedi academy.

He shut down the muffled twin ion engines and opened the cockpit door, heaving himself out. Reaching into the stowage compartment behind his pilot's seat, he retrieved the pack of supplies that contained all the explosives he would need for a full day's work. . . .

Orvak stepped on the squishing, plant-covered ground. The jungle brooded around him, chaotic and threatening. Overhead, he could hear the crackling hum of the energy shield that had destroyed his partner.

Compared with the clean, sterile Shadow Academy, Yavin 4 felt disgustingly *alive*. It swarmed with vermin, plants growing everywhere, little rodents, insects, strange biting creatures that moved in every direction and hid in every cranny.

He longed for the precise and spotless corridors of the Shadow Academy, where his boots could ring loud and clear on the cold, hard metal plates, where he could smell the recycled air flowing through the ventilators, where everything was regimented and in its rightful place . . . just as the Empire would be again after its victory over the Rebels. Orvak took comfort in his solid leather gloves and the helmet that protected him from infestation by the parasitic creatures of this uncivilized world.

Taking the pack that contained his demolition equipment, he sprinted away from his TIE fighter toward the humming shield generator station. It hulked over him, powerful and unguarded. Doomed.

Although the shield generators were obviously new, vines, creepers, and ferns grew in tangled profusion close to the warm machinery. Orvak could see hacked ends and broken branches where someone had chopped away the foliage in an attempt to keep the access clear. The irresistible jungle, though, kept pressing its advantage. Orvak shook his head at the folly of these Rebels.

When he reached the pulsing station, Orvak hunched over and glanced from side to side, expecting Rebel defenders at any moment. Opening his pack, he withdrew two of his six high-powered thermal detonators, shaped charges he would place against the generator's power cells. These two explosives would be sufficient to take down the Jedi academy's shields.

He would save the rest of the explosives for the second part of his mission.

Orvak synchronized the timers. Then, removing his recalibrated compass and glancing at the coordinates he had programmed in, he ducked and fought his way through the underbrush toward his next target, which was some distance through the jungle and across a river.

The Great Temple.

He paused for only a moment, opaquing his blast goggles as the timers ran down to zero—and the explosive charges detonated.

The boom was deafening, and a pillar of fire rose to the sky, singeing the surrounding Massassi trees. Satisfied, Orvak congratulated himself on an excellent explosion. Most spectacular.

But the next one would be better yet.

4

WITH RAYNAR AND Tionne crowded in the back, Lowie piloted the T-23 skyhopper back toward the Jedi academy at full speed. As they skimmed along the treetops, Lowie explained the situation as best he could, with Em Teedee translating.

". . . and that is why Master Skywalker requested that Master Lowbacca retrieve you with such haste," the little droid finished.

"Well, well, well," Raynar said in a sour voice. "I suppose you think this is going to make you heroes for coming back to save the Jedi academy. I'm sure *I* could have managed quite nicely without your help. While you were off playing, I was here training with Tionne."

Lowie could tell by the blond-haired boy's tone of voice that he was none too pleased to be stuffed unceremoniously into the cramped rear seat, with his brightly colored robes tangled about him. Raynar's parents had once been minor royalty on Alderaan, before that planet was destroyed by the Death Star, and now they had made themselves into wealthy merchants. He was not accustomed to taking a backseat to anyone.

"No, Raynar," Tionne chided. The silvery-haired Jedi teacher blinked her alien mother-of-pearl eyes. "No one does as well alone against an enemy, and we must all work together to prepare. Without preparation, a battle is all but lost."

Raynar snorted, trying to straighten his robes. "Battle? We don't even know there's going to *be* a battle. Why should we believe the word of some traitor boy who's gone over to the dark side? He could just be lying to get us all worked up. He's probably laughing at us right now."

Lowie's growls rumbled louder than the engine of the T-23. "Master Lowbacca wishes to point out," Em Teedee said, "that for many years Zekk was a close friend to Master Jacen and Mistress Jaina."

Raynar pouted. "Then Jacen and Jaina Solo need to be more careful about the friends they choose."

"Sometimes," Tionne said in a firm voice, "the gap between friend and enemy is not as wide as you may think. Help often comes from unexpected sources."

Lowie wasn't sure why, but senses in the back of his mind urged him to go faster still. The small skyhopper shuddered and dipped as he pushed its engines to their limits, and then beyond. He flew in among the trees, below the deadly dome of the energy shield that protected the Jedi academy against an attack from the skies.

"Hey, watch out for that big branch!" Raynar yelped as Lowie swerved to one side. "Save the heroics for when the Shadow Academy shows up—*if* they come, that is." Lowie was pleased to sense, though, that Tionne not only remained calm, but actually approved of the way he piloted the little T-23.

Lowie looked up into the sky and understood why he had felt the sudden need to accelerate. He gave a sharp bark, pointing up at the ominous spiked ring shape barely visible as a silhouette through the film of the atmosphere. "Master Lowbacca says—oh dear!—it seems that the Shadow Academy has arrived!"

Raynar fell silent, finding nothing more to criticize about Lowie's piloting. Before long, a blade of piercing sound sliced through the silence, followed by several explosions. According to Lowie's sensors, the flickering energy shield above had failed. He growled out the news.

Without waiting for a translation, Tionne said, "We can still return to the Jedi academy, but we should leave the T-23 at the edge of the jungle. I have a feeling it's not safe to approach the temple landing field or the hangar bay. It's bound to be under attack." She sat up straight between the two young Jedi trainees. "It has already begun."

The Great Temple of the Massassi had stood nearly unchanged for thousands of years. The stone blocks in the walls and floors were as solid as they had been the day they were assembled. Even so, Jaina felt a vibration in the floor of the Jedi academy's control center. Warning lights flashed across the shield generator console.

"Something's wrong, Uncle Luke," Jaina said. "There's been an explosion out in the jungle . . . oh no! Our defensive shields are down!"

Luke stood behind the chair where Jacen sat at the communications controls. He nodded grimly to Jaina. "Can you get the shields back on line from here?"

She frantically flicked switches and checked connections, trying to bring the shields back up. She scanned the display screens and diagnostics, continually pushing buttons. "Don't think so," she replied. "Power's out. The entire generator might be gone."

Her brother Jacen blew out his breath and pushed back from the comm console. "I've got a bad feeling about this," he said, running fingers through his tousled brown curls. "I'll bet it's sabotage."

Luke caught Jaina's eyes, then Jacen's, and came to a decision. "I'm calling an all-hands meeting in five minutes. We may need to clear out the Great Temple, go into hiding in the jungles where we can deflect the assault. Send a message to your mother that we're under attack *now* and need those reinforcements right away. Then meet me in the grand audience chamber."

Jacen looked at his sister in a state of near panic. "My animals . . ." he said. "I *can't* leave them in their cages if the Jedi academy's under attack. They'll stand a better chance of surviving if they're free.

And if Uncle Luke's going to evacuate all of the students—"

"Go ahead," Jaina said, waving him away. "Take care of your pets. I'll get a message to Mom."

Already running for the door, Jacen tossed a "thank you" over his shoulder.

Jaina plopped down at the comm station, selected a transmission frequency, and tried to make a connection to Coruscant. She received no response, only dead static. With a sigh of disgust over the erratic behavior of the old equipment, Jaina tried a new frequency.

Still nothing.

Odd, she thought. Maybe the main comm screen wasn't working. She donned the headset and selected yet another frequency.

Static. She switched again. Stronger static, as if something had swallowed up her desperate signal. Soon the crackling hiss built to a crescendo squeal loud enough to set her teeth on edge. Jaina snatched the headset off her ears and tossed it down with a shudder.

"We're being jammed!"

Jaina checked the readouts on the communications console just to be sure. Their long-range transmissions were being blocked by the Shadow Academy.

She had to let Luke know right away.

· · ·

In his chambers inside the ancient temple, Jacen lifted the latches and slid aside the doors to each cage that held his menagerie of unusual pets. He could see that Tionne had kept them well fed while he was gone on Kashyyyk. The near-invisible crystal snake with its iridescent scales glittered with languid satisfaction, but the family of purple jumping spiders in the adjoining cage bounced up and down in agitation.

"It's all right," Jacen sent the message with his mind. "Be calm. You'll be safe if you get to the jungle. Just get into the jungle."

One cage rattled with two clamoring stintarils, tree-dwelling rodents with protruding eyes and long jaws filled with sharp teeth. In another damp enclosure tiny swimming crabs peeked out of their mud nests. Pinkish mucous salamanders slid out of their water bowl, gradually taking a distinct form. Iridescent blue piranha-beetles swarmed against the tough wires of their cage, chewing and eager to be free.

He turned them loose one by one, carrying them to the window as carefully as he could, moving with a controlled urgency. Jacen had just set the last of his creatures free—his favorite, a stump lizard—when he heard a loud Wookiee roar, followed by the voice of Em Teedee.

"Oh, thank goodness, we're not alone in the temple after all."

Jacen turned to find Lowie, Em Teedee, Tionne, and Raynar standing in his doorway.

"Did the others leave without us?" Raynar asked with a look of forlorn worry on his face.

"Everyone's up in the grand audience chamber," Jacen said. "We need to get there as quickly as possible. Master Skywalker's giving his final instructions before the battle begins."

When the group stepped out of the turbolift into the grand audience chamber, Jaina was already there talking in a low voice with Luke and Tenel Ka while the other students sat in frightened silence.

A look of relief washed over Luke's face when he saw that Lowie had returned successfully from his mission. Tionne stretched out her hand toward Luke, and he gave it a brief squeeze.

"I'm glad you're safe," Luke said.

"What did Mom say?" Jacen asked his sister.

Jaina bit her lower lip, and Tenel Ka

answered for her. "The Shadow Academy is jamming our transmissions. We were unable to send our distress signal."

Jacen felt the blood drain out of his face. How long would it be, then, until reinforcements arrived, if they couldn't even send a distress call?

Luke spoke in a loud voice, addressing the gathered Jedi students. "We can't rely on outside help to save us. We must fight this battle ourselves. I believe the Great Temple will be the initial target of attack. Tenel Ka has already briefed you on ground tactics, so we're going to move this battle to the jungle—where the territory will be new for the Shadow Academy's troops, but familiar to us. We'll fight them one-on-one.

"But we must evacuate the Jedi academy immediately."

5

FROM THE SHADOW Academy's crowded hangar bay, Zekk watched the final preparations for the attack. The frenzy of bustling troops, mixed with their brooding anger and lust for destruction, galvanized him. He felt as if the lines of Force around him had been set on fire.

The hub of the activity was an immense hovering battle platform that dominated the hangar bay. Constructed specifically for this most important assault on the Rebel Alliance, the movable tactical platform bristled with weaponry. Stormtroopers crawled over its armored surface, preparing to launch. Guided by the ominous Nightsister Tamith Kai, the platform would be the staging point for the ground combat, Jedi versus Jedi.

At the battle platform's helm she stood, eager for vengeance. Her long black cape slithered around her with a hissing sound, like snakes coming out to strike. Spines, taken from the carapace of a murderous giant insect, protruded from her shoulders. Her black hair curled around her head like ebony wires, writhing and crackling with dark powers, each strand seemingly alive and malevolent.

Tamith Kai's violet eyes burned as she ordered the stormtroopers to board the battle platform, gathering her inner power. Her onyx-scaled armor clung to her muscular, well-formed body. Her demeanor spoke of power and confidence—and a yearning for destruction.

Zekk tended to his own duties. He himself had been a target of Tamith Kai's suspicious thoughts. The Nightsister didn't trust him. She felt that his commitment to the dark side wasn't strong enough, that he was blinded by his former friendship with the Jedi twins, Jacen and Jaina Solo.

Zekk had been trained as the prize student of Lord Brakiss, and had defeated the Nightsister's own protégé Vilas in a duel to the death. By winning the duel, Zekk had gained the title of Darkest Knight. And Tamith Kai—perhaps because she was simply a sore loser, or perhaps because she sensed his flickering doubts—rarely let him out of her sight.

But Brakiss had given *him* command of the Shadow Academy's new Force-wielders who would be the vanguard of the battle to reclaim the galaxy. He himself would lead the Dark Jedi strike force, dropping like death from the skies to obliterate Master Skywalker's trainees.

Zekk drew a deep breath, smelled the metallic tang in the cold air. He heard coolants pumping, engines powering up, the clatter of stormtrooper armor, preparatory signals as systems were locked down. They were ready to launch.

Zekk turned to his group of Force-talented warriors. He wore his crimson-lined black cape and his leather armor; his lightsaber hung clipped at his side, waiting to be used. He had secured his long dark hair in a neat ponytail, and his emerald-green eyes flashed at those gathered around him.

"Feel the Force move through you," he said to the other trainees. They stood with their jaws set, their eyes alert, eager for battle. They had been trained for this.

He gestured to the waiting platform, and the Dark Jedi moved with a fluid motion as they entered the armored vessel. "We must strike the Jedi academy now, before we lose our element of surprise."

• • •

The TIE pilot's helmet fit perfectly on his gray-haired head. Along with the breathing mask, goggles, black flight suit, padded gloves, and heavy boots, the uniform seemed to transport Qorl back to a different time, a time when he had been much younger . . . a pilot for the first Empire.

Years ago, he had flown with his wing of TIE fighters from the original Death Star to attack the desperate fleet of Rebel X-wings. He had been shot down in combat, spiralling down to crash-land in the wilds of Yavin 4. When he had looked behind him, to his absolute horror and disbelief Qorl had watched the invincible Death Star blow up, leaving him stranded on the miserable little moon.

After recovering from his injuries, Qorl had lived like a hermit for over twenty years until four young Jedi trainees had stumbled upon him . . . setting in motion the events that had returned him to the Second Imperium.

And now, Qorl found himself boarding another TIE fighter, launching from another battle station—once more ready to defeat the Rebels. This time, though, he was sure it would end differently. This time the Empire would make no mistakes.

Qorl stood in front of his wing of twelve TIE fighters. Crowded into the side of the launching bay, the small fighters would take off as soon as the battle platform descended. He turned to his troops, all of them unproven fighters, taken from the ranks of the most ambitious new stormtrooper trainees. The new pilots had never seen combat. They had only practiced, performing simulation after simulation—but he knew they were itching for a real fight. The pilots stood beside their ships, clothed in identical black flight suits and helmets.

One new pilot fidgeted with obvious eagerness, glancing toward his TIE fighter, studying the laser cannon turrets, anxious to be off. He finally stepped forward. The fighter removed his helmet and held it against his chest. Even before seeing the young man's wide face, though, Qorl knew it was the broad-shouldered Norys, former leader of the Lost Ones gang.

"Excuse me, sir—I have a suggestion," Norys said. "In light of my superior performance during the simulations, since I scored better than any of these others, I think I should be the one to lead this wing."

Qorl quelled his anger. "I . . . understand your reasons, Norys. You have done excellent work in your cross-training as a TIE pilot and stormtrooper. You are eager to learn and, presumably, to *serve* the Second Imperium. But I must turn down your request this time."

"On what basis?"

Sensing the challenge in the young man's voice, Qorl kept his answer firm and direct. "On the basis that Brakiss chose me to command this mission. If you prefer not to follow orders, however . . ." He shrugged, leaving the implication hanging in the air between them.

The boy was rude and so often insubordinate that if he hadn't shown such a true aptitude for weaponry and fighting skills, Qorl would certainly have left him behind. Too much was at stake in this mission to allow an overeager young man to botch things up.

Norys flushed. "I think *you* are afraid, Qorl. You're old and haven't flown a mission in years. You're leading the wing so you can hold us back to cover your own failures."

"That will be all," Qorl said in a voice that, although quiet, was so commanding that the air cracked with tension. "I give you the choice: say the word and I'll ground you from this mission, or hold your tongue and fight for your Emperor." At the moment Qorl didn't care what the surly young man chose. He would gladly take a smaller fighting wing if it was the only way to ensure that all his pilots were well disciplined.

Fuming, Norys struggled to keep silent and rammed the black helmet back onto his head.

Qorl spoke, more to divert attention from the outburst than for any other reason. "We have successfully jammed all signals from the Jedi academy. They are unable to call for reinforcements. Since no battleships are in orbit, the foolish Jedi Knights must have assumed that their own powers and their puny energy shield would be enough to thwart us.

"According to our monitoring systems, our first Imperial commando raid has already succeeded in removing their shields. The Jedi academy lies open and vulnerable to our attack.

"When Tamith Kai launches her battle platform to guide the military strike, Lord Zekk will take his Dark Jedi trainees and combat the Jedi Knights directly. Our wing will fly harassment strikes from the air. Although we are meant to cause considerable damage, our mission is to *support*, not to serve as the front line of attack. Is that understood?"

The pilots murmured their understanding. Qorl couldn't tell if Norys's voice had joined them.

"Very well. To your ships," he said.

His pilots scrambled into their cockpits, and Qorl settled in behind the pilot's controls of the lead TIE fighter. He drew a deep breath through the filtering mask, smelling the delicious and familiar chemical taint of the air from his tanks.

He smiled. It felt so good to be able to fly once again.

From the helm of the tactical battle platform Tamith Kai shouted, "Let us be off. We shall return victorious before this day is done!"

The great hangar bay doors opened, revealing the blackness of space shared with the emerald moon, behind which loomed the boiling orange cauldron of the gas giant Yavin. The moon looked insignificant against the panorama of the universe—but it was the Shadow Academy's target, destined to become the site of a furious battle and an Imperial victory.

Tamith Kai commanded the battle platform to rise up on its repulsorlifts and head out of the Shadow Academy. The military vessel appeared to be a large, flattened sailbarge with rounded corners, two levels high, with an upper command deck that would open to the air once they reached the atmosphere. Armed stormtroopers and ground assault forces filled the first level, while Zekk and his Dark Jedi took their positions in the bottom bay near the drop doors.

The battle platform descended through space toward the thin fingernail of atmosphere around the green moon. As the minutes passed, Zekk paced back and forth. He looked out the viewports and saw the ring station high overhead, dwindling as the battle platform increased speed toward Yavin 4.

"Packs ready?" he asked, adjusting the equipment strapped across his chest and back. His black cape hung over it, its scarlet inner lining flashing as he moved. His squad of Dark Jedi checked their weapons, scores of identical lightsabers manufactured aboard the Shadow Academy. The team members adjusted their repulsorpacks on their shoulders. One by one they declared their readiness.

The blackness of space was streaked with white haze as the battle platform plunged headfirst into the atmosphere. Zekk felt a buffeting vibration as the winds clawed the armored plates.

The hull heated up, and Zekk could sense the ionized scream of the shockwave through the air, but Tamith Kai piloted the battle platform expertly, without hesitation, directly toward their target.

The Nightsister's deep, hard voice came over the comm. "We're approaching target altitude. Zekk, prepare your Dark Jedi for departure. The air-drop doors will open in one standard minute."

Zekk clapped his gloved hands, ordering the Dark Jedi to stand in ranks. "The repulsorpacks will carry you," he said, "but use your Force abilities to guide your descent. We must strike directly. These are our sworn enemies, Luke Skywalker's Jedi Knights. The future of the galaxy hinges on our victory today."

Zekk fixed his penetrating gaze on each one of the trainees, trying to impart a fraction of his determination to them. They were valiant warriors, vowing to succeed in their quest.

But Zekk had not yet dealt with his own

inner turmoil. He knew in his heart that Tamith Kai's doubts about his loyalty had a legitimate foundation—he *did* feel a longing friendship toward his dear friend Jaina Solo and her brother Jacen.

Deep in the forests of Kashyyyk he had warned Jaina to stay away from the Jedi academy. He did not want her to be part of this battle today. He did not want her to become a victim.

But he knew with equal certainty that the Jaina Solo he knew and cared for would never stay away to save herself and leave her friends to die. He dreaded the thought that she might be down there ready to fight against him.

Zekk was grateful to have his thoughts interrupted as the floor thumped and the drop-bay doors creaked open. A line of brighter air like a thin, toothless smile appeared at their feet and then yawned wide. The jungle treetops were visible below, punctuated by the protruding stone towers of ancient Massassi temples.

"All right, my Dark Jedi," Zekk shouted into the howling wind. "The hour is ours. Depart!" Leading the charge, he dove into the sky, switched on his repulsorpack, and tumbled toward the unprotected Jedi academy.

Behind him the other Dark Jedi dropped from the battle platform one by one, falling like deadly birds of prey.

In flight Zekk ignited his lightsaber, holding it out like a glowing beacon. He glanced up to see the other assault troops similarly extending their blazing weapons, capes fluttering behind them.

Dark Jedi rained down from the sky.

6

THE SHRIEK OF twin ion engines ripped apart the relative quiet of the grand audience chamber. Tenel Ka's reflexes took over even before she recognized the source of the sound, and she found herself running in a crouch toward the closest window slit, with Jaina, Jacen, and Lowbacca right beside her. Through the slit in the stone wall, Tenel Ka saw TIE fighters on a strafing run—coming straight toward the Jedi academy!

"Master Skywalker, we are under attack," Tenel Ka shouted.

Luke Skywalker raised his voice to be heard throughout the chamber. "Everyone, stay in the jungles until the battle is over. Fight with all your skills and abilities. Remember your training . . . and may the Force be with you."

A series of hollow-sounding explosions punctuated his command. A loud *crack!* echoed through the chamber as a proton bomb struck the lowermost levels and dug a crater in the jungle soil outside the pyramid.

From where she stood, Tenel Ka observed the other Jedi trainees and judged that their reactions to Master Skywalker's orders were commendable. Several students gasped in surprise, and Tenel Ka could sense conflicting emotions—nervous anticipation, homesickness, trust in the Force, dread at the possibility of having to kill. But she caught no hint of confusion, panic, or denial.

Without waiting for further instructions, Jedi students streamed out of the grand audience chamber. Luke Skywalker dashed to the window where Tenel Ka's group stood and motioned for Peckhum to join them. The old spacer ducked as stone powder fell from the ceiling, shaken loose by the pounding from above.

The Jedi Master began issuing instructions immediately, and Tenel Ka marveled at how calm he seemed in the midst of the turmoil. "Jacen, take the *Shadow Chaser* into orbit. See if you can break through the jamming signal and send a message to your mother that we're under attack. Artoo-Detoo's down in the hangar bay already waiting with the ship. He's all the copilot you'll need."

Jaina, who loved to fly, was about to protest

when Luke turned to her. "I need you to go across the river and check out the shield generator equipment. See if there's any chance of getting our defensive shields back up. Lowie, I want you and Tenel Ka—" The comlink clipped to Luke's belt interrupted him, signaling an urgent message.

Another explosion vibrated through the Great Temple, this one closer than the others. As soon as Luke switched on his comlink, Artoo-Detoo's alarmed bleeps and whistles issued from it.

"What's that, Artoo? Calm down," Luke said.

"If you would allow me, Master Skywalker," Em Teedee said, "I was able to parse your astromech droid's message and could provide a translation for you. I am fluent in over six forms of communic—"

"Thank you, Em Teedee," Luke Skywalker cut off the little droid's chatter, "that would be very helpful."

"Artoo-Detoo reports that—oh dear!—the front of the hangar bay has been hit. Rubble has completely sealed off the entrance. No ships can get in or out. The *Shadow Chaser* is trapped inside."

"Hey," Jacen said after a moment of

thought, "Peckhum, what about the *Lightning Rod*? It's not sealed in."

Tenel Ka felt a frown crease her forehead at the thought of Jacen facing an Imperial attack in the rickety old cargo shuttle.

"The *Lightning Rod* doesn't have the *Shadow Chaser*'s quantum armor," Luke pointed out.

"Too dangerous," Jaina said.

"Hey, we're *all* in danger here," Jacen said in a low, firm voice. "And we have to get a message out."

"Sure, we could do it," old Peckhum said. "I've learned some pretty good evasive maneuvers in my day—enough to make it to orbit without gettin' blown up, I'd guess."

Just then Lowbacca gave a warning yelp and pointed toward the window slit. Hovering over the jungle in the distance was an ominous-looking construction, a giant weapon-studded tactical platform, like a deadly raft carrying enemy troops.

Tenel Ka felt a stab of recognition. "Tamith Kai is there; I can feel her," she said.

"It looks like she's directing the ground battle from up there," Luke said.

"Then we must disable that battle platform," Tenel Ka replied without a pause. "I volunteer. The Nightsister is mine."

Lowbacca barked a comment. "Master Lowbacca wishes to point out that his T-23 is still out near the landing pad. Using the skyhopper, he and Mistress Tenel Ka could easily reach that platform within minutes."

Luke nodded. "We each have our missions. I'll do one last sweep of the pyramid to make sure no one was left behind. I'll see you all out at the rendezvous point in the jungle."

As the young Jedi Knights raced down the stairs inside the temple, Tenel Ka's mind already began moving ahead to the coming confrontation. Adrenaline pumped through her veins, and her mind was alert. She had been bred and trained for battle.

Although fighting with only one arm would present her with new challenges, she felt neither afraid nor overconfident. She was simply *ready*. A Jedi must always be ready, she knew. Master Skywalker and Tionne had trained them all well. Tenel Ka had her lightsaber and her Force skills. Together, she was certain, that was enough for her to defeat any enemy.

By the time they all reached the landing pad, Jaina had already split off from the group, plunging toward the river and the shield generator station. Tenel Ka was surprised to note that the old pilot Peckhum had kept up with them as he and Jacen sprinted toward the battered supply shuttle.

Dodging energy bolts from the TIE fighters that swooped overhead, Tenel Ka and Lowbacca scrambled into the T-23 skyhopper while Peckhum and Jacen boarded the *Lightning Rod*.

Watching Jacen run up the ramp into the *Lightning Rod*, Tenel Ka felt a tug at her emotions she could not explain, even to herself. Almost at the same moment, Jacen reappeared and stared at Tenel Ka with a serious expression. His face broke into a grin. "I'll tell you a joke when we get back—a good one this time." Then he was gone again.

As Lowie fired up the T-23's repulsorjets, Tenel Ka answered, though she knew he couldn't hear her, "Yes, my friend Jacen, I would like to hear your joke. When we all get back."

7

THE *LIGHTNING ROD*'S engines whined as the ship strained against gravity. Just after liftoff, the battered vessel gave a sharp jolt. Alarm bells went off inside Jacen's head. "We're hit!" he cried, not even bothering to check the readouts.

"Naw," old Peckhum answered. "*Lightning Rod*'s been doin' that ever since I switched out the power coupling to the rear repulsorjets. I guess I'll have to take a look at that again one of these days."

The knot of panic in Jacen's stomach eased a little—but only a little. "Maybe Jaina can help you with it later," he said.

An energy bolt streaked by as a TIE fighter sang past them on its descent toward the Jedi academy. "Hey, that was a close one!" Jacen said.

"Too close," Peckhum agreed. "Hang on, young Solo—I'm gonna try some evasive maneuvers."

• • •

Lowie focused his full concentration on getting the T-23 to cover. With his peripheral vision he could see other Jedi students dodging fire from TIE fighters as they sprinted for the safety of the trees. When they reached the edge of the forest, the young Wookiee pulled his skyhopper into a sharp climb.

The dense network of leafy branches had always signified protection to Lowie, and he longed for a few peaceful moments in the treetops. But no peace awaited Lowie and Tenel Ka up there. Not this time.

Lowie clenched the steering controls tightly and zigzagged the flight path across the treetops, trying to throw off any pursuers who might be on their track. Today trouble rained down on them from above, and he could flee to no safe height. His best bet lay in remaining among the trees.

An energy bolt spat past the T-23 and sent up a plume of dirt and singed turf behind them. "Let the Force guide you, Lowbacca, my friend," Tenel Ka said from the passenger seat in back.

Lowie rumbled an acknowledgment and took a deep calming breath. He flew onward, letting the Force control his weaving and dodging. They headed toward the wide, greenish-brown river over which Tenel Ka and Lowbacca had seen the Nightsister's sinister battle platform. Even from half a kilometer away, they could see lances of laser fire shoot out from the armored vessel, incinerating trees along the banks.

Suddenly, Tenel Ka gave a shout of surprise. "Look. There!"

From the sky above a group of figures descended like swooping birds of prey— human forms. Dark Jedi dropped from the clouds in a dispersed attack pattern, lightsabers flashing as they controlled their direction with repulsorpacks.

A proximity alarm sounded the moment Lowbacca diverted his attention, and a laser cannon blast from a passing TIE fighter struck them. A jet of smoke and sparks spewed from the T-23's rear engines. The tiny skyhopper shimmied and bucked in the air. With a shriek of shearing metal, one of the attitude-control fins gave way.

"Oh my," Em Teedee wailed. "I can't bear to watch."

Lowie, reacting with the instinct of his Jedi training, wrestled with the controls. Directed by the Force, one of his sharp-clawed hands flew across the control panel, while his free hand guided their descent. Smoke poured into the cockpit, and the skyhopper sputtered and rocked. Without knowing quite how he did it, Lowie cut the rear engines and bled off their momentum into a steep upward climb. Then, letting the little ship fall back toward the treetops, he used one final burst from the repulsorjets to slow their descent—enough, he hoped.

The T-23 crashed onto the jungle canopy.

With every breath, Tenel Ka drew fire into her aching lungs. Nearby a Wookiee groaned, but she could not make sense of the growled words. She could see nothing.

"Mistress Tenel Ka!" A strident electronic voice broke into her foggy consciousness. "Master Lowbacca urgently requests your assistance removing the T-23's canopy."

Tenel Ka tried to look around. She saw only roiling, changing shapes of light and dark. The shifting patterns stung her eyes, and she squeezed them tightly shut.

A voice loud enough to wake a Jedi Master from a healing trance wailed in Tenel Ka's ears. "Oh, curse my sluggish processor, I'm too late. She's dead!"

Lowbacca bellowed a loud denial. At the

same time, something reached out and gave her a sharp nudge.

"No," Tenel Ka managed to croak. "I'm alive."

Lowbacca gave a few crisp barks, and Tenel Ka found herself responding to his instructions even before Em Teedee could clarify, "Master Lowbacca asks you to push against the canopy with all your might whilst throwing your weight toward the port side—to the left, you know."

Tenel Ka knew. She pushed and rocked. Despite the choking clouds of smoke from the burning engines, she grew calm enough to let the Force flow through her.

Even through her closed eyelids, Tenel Ka could tell when Em Teedee switched on the bright yellow beams of his optical sensors to cut through the smoke. "It would seem," the little droid went on, "that the T-23's canopy is wedged against a tree branch. Oh, we're doomed!"

Then, just as the little droid finished his lament, the skyhopper's canopy popped free, and fresh air flooded the cockpit. Both Tenel Ka and Lowbacca stripped out of their crash webbing and scrambled free of the wreckage. As they moved away from the smoldering craft, panting for breath and waiting for their vision to clear, Tenel Ka's hand went automatically to her lightsaber to be sure it was still clipped firmly at her waist. It was.

"Oh dear," Em Teedee exclaimed in a tinny voice. "Now we'll most likely become lost in the jungle and captured by woolamanders. Do be careful, Master Lowbacca. I should hate to repeat that dreadful experience."

Balancing on a tree limb beside Tenel Ka, Lowbacca turned to gaze at the crashed T-23 and uttered a low, mournful note. Tenel Ka could see that his distress came not from the thought of jungle creatures, but from the loss of his beloved vehicle. The warrior girl understood loss. She reached out her single hand to touch Lowbacca's arm briefly and let the strength of the Force comfort him. Then, as one, they turned to seek out their destination: the giant battle platform— and the evil Nightsister.

To Kenel Ka's relief and surprise, Lowbacca had managed to crash-land barely two hundred meters from where the battle platform hovered above the crowns of the Massassi trees. Before she could speak, though, her Wookiee friend gave a low woof of warning and pointed downward toward cover.

Tenel Ka understood immediately and scrambled down into the leaves and branches until she was hidden. If they could see the giant battle platform, then they themselves could be seen. They would need to make their way to the battle platform *beneath* the rippling green leaves, like swimmers below the surface of an ocean.

With only one arm to help her balance and pull herself along, Tenel Ka had to trust the Force to place her feet securely at each step. She even welcomed Lowbacca's help when he offered it in crossing weak branches or broad gaps.

Tenel Ka wasn't sure why she felt compelled to speak. Perhaps it was the air of sadness that hung about her Wookiee friend. "We will spend many enjoyable days repairing your T-23, Lowbacca my friend—you, Jacen, Jaina, and I. After this battle is over."

The Wookiee stopped, looked at her quizzically for a moment, then chuffed with laughter. After a series of woofs, Em Teedee said, "Master Lowbacca adds that Master Jacen will most likely be delighted to have a captive audience to entertain with his jokes."

Tenel Ka felt her own spirits brighten at

that thought, and they moved forward at a more rapid pace. Her mind focused on the goal of defeating the Second Imperium once and for all.

Suddenly, she felt a tingle run up her spine. "Halt!" she said. A TIE fighter swooped low across the leaves, rippling the canopy around them with its hot exhaust as it circled to inspect the crashed skyhopper. Lowbacca growled, and Tenel Ka held his arm to restrain him from any rash action. The Imperial ship circled again over the wreckage, as if looking for survivors. Tenel Ka hoped the pilot wouldn't blast the already-downed craft into a smoldering lump of slag and debris. After a tense moment, the enemy ship roared away in search of new prey.

She and Lowbacca pressed on through the trees toward where the battle platform waited.

It seemed like no time at all before Em Teedee said, "Unless my senses have become completely uncalibrated by the crash, we should be directly below the leading edge of the battle platform right now."

Lowbacca held out a hand, motioning for Tenel Ka to wait, and scrambled up a few branches to check their location. At his low bark of triumph, she climbed after him and pushed her head above the leafy canopy. There, hovering ten meters over the tree-tops, was the underside of the giant battle platform, massive and threatening, armored for assault, bristling with weapons.

"It should be a simple enough task to destroy it," Tenel Ka said.

The sounds of shouted orders and clomping booted feet carried down to them. Lowbacca pointed upward and then shrugged as if to say, What next? The platform was too high above the trees to make a jump, and they had no repulsorpacks of their own. Tenel Ka reached for the grappling hook and fibercord she kept at her belt.

"We'll have to climb for it," she said.

The platform hovered higher than Tenel Ka was accustomed to aiming, but the grappling hook caught firmly on the armored edge on her second throw. Tenel Ka tested her weight on the fibercord. The grappling hook did not budge. Then, wrapping her arm and her legs around the cord, she began to climb, using the Force to help levitate her when her single arm couldn't provide enough support.

Above on the platform waited Imperial

stormtroopers, heavy armaments, and a Nightsister from Dathomir.

Tenel Ka swallowed hard. She knew that although the Force was with them, the *odds* definitely were not.

8

THE GREEN-BROWN RIVER that flowed sluggishly through the primeval forest was broad and powerful, yet outwardly calm. The current showed not the least bit of disturbance from the titanic struggle of good and evil taking place on Yavin 4.

The river hosted numerous life-forms: invisible plankton and carnivorous protozoans, water plants, trees that dangled sharp roots into the flow, and camouflaged predators that disguised themselves as innocuous parts of the landscape.

But as blaster shots rang out and the buzz of lightsabers droned through the jungle, other creatures moved in the thick branches over the river and in the water itself . . . creatures trained in using the Force.

Rounded reptilian snouts broke the surface of the murky river. Breathing slits rose up, nostrils flaring to draw in welcome oxygen. The three scaly creatures moved slowly enough that only slight ripples whispered across the water. Settling into position deep in the mud, they sniffed and lay in wait near the path at the river's edge.

Their enemies would come soon.

Moving stealthily yet radiating a supremely confident power, three of the Dark Jedi trainees from the Shadow Academy strode through the underbrush, hacking away the dense vines and branches with their lightsaber blades. They reached the riverbank and paused to consult with each other, still searching for their opponents.

"Skywalker's Jedi trainees are cowards," one said. "Why don't they come out and fight? They all hide in the jungle like terrified rodents."

"How can they not be afraid of us?" another one said. "They know the power of the dark side."

Consulting silently, with only a faint stream of bubble for communication, three of Luke Skywalker's reptilian Cha'a trainees lunged out of the river, spewing a stream of water at their enemies. They used the Force to summon a hammering flow of the river, a column of drenching wetness that reared up like a snake, then splashed down. The Dark Jedi lightsaber blades sizzled and steamed.

The three Cha'a hissed and chattered with laughter as they summoned up more and more water.

The watcrlogged Dark Jedi sputtered and thrashed from side to side as they attempted to summon up dark-side powers with which to strike back at their reptilian opponents.

Just then, from the dense shelter of the trees above, a trio of feathered avians left their perches and plunged down. They let out a high, fluting whistle of a battle cry.

The Dark Jedi were distracted for a moment, torn between two enemies. Then the avians landed on top of them, driving them to the ground and knocking them unconscious. The avians chirped and screeched in victory as the Cha'a hauled themselves dripping out of the river mud and slogged toward the three new captives.

Working together, Skywalker's alien Jedi trainees removed whiplike vines from the underbrush and lashed the arms and legs of their prisoners together. One of the Cha'a picked up the discarded Shadow Academy lightsabers, studied the poor construction and unimaginative workmanship. One by one, he tossed the tainted weapons into the river. They splashed, and sank without a trace.

Meanwhile, the avians crouched over the unconscious captives and used their Jedi powers to probe the minds of Brakiss's students. They added strong Force suggestions to make sure their enemies would continue to sleep for a long time. . . .

Tionne tossed her long silvery-white hair behind her to get it out of the way. She would need her vision unobstructed, with no distractions.

She looked at the other Jedi students with her gleaming mother-of-pearl eyes. Master Skywalker frequently entrusted her with training these students, and now Tionne would do battle. The Yavin 4 academy had often been a target of the forces of evil—but the true Jedi Knights had won before, and she had no doubt they would win again.

She and her students stood around the flat marble slab and broken columns of what had once been an open-air Massassi temple before it was swallowed up by the jungle. This was the place at which they had chosen to make their stand.

"Are you all ready?" Tionne said. "Remember what you have been taught. *There is no try.* We must succeed in defeating the warriors of the dark side."

Her students shouted their agreement, looking at her with eyes full of confidence in their abilities and her plan. One of the young women nodded to Tionne, took a deep breath, then ran off into the forest in search of the invading Dark Jedi. Within only moments the young woman cried out, shouting, challenging the trainees of the Shadow Academy.

Tionne heard a lightsaber sizzle. Branches fell . . . and then came the sound of footsteps crashing through the forest as her student hurried back toward the trap they had set. Tionne gestured silently for the others to prepare themselves.

"Come back here, Jedi vermin!" one of the enemy called, hidden by the thickets.

Four Dark Jedi came plunging through the jungles, bursting into the temple clearing where the panting student stood on the other side of a flat marble slab hanging above their heads. Tionne's student looked defeated.

The invaders stepped forward. "We will crush your mind with the dark side!" one said.

"Now!" Tionne shouted. From their shadowy hiding places, four of her special students reached out with the Force: in an unexpected, irresistible move, they snatched the four lightsabers from enemy hands. The Dark Jedi cried out in alarm and surprise at losing their weapons. Then Tionne and her students emerged from the underbrush and surrounded them.

"We don't need our lightsabers to defeat you. We can still flatten you with our power!" said the first overconfident opponent. "The power of the dark side!" All four of the enemy Jedi stood in a tight cluster, back to back, raising their hands.

"I wouldn't do that if I were you," Tionne said calmly, letting her pale lips show a brief smile. "You wouldn't want to distract us—a brief fluctuation in our concentration might become a *crushing* defeat for you."

She glanced upward. Her four students remained motionless with their eyes closed, focused on their task.

The Dark Jedi looked up and saw that the marble slab they had thought to be the ceiling of a crumbling temple was completely unsupported, a hovering rectangle of rock weighing many tons, balanced over their heads. It floated, held up by nothing but the power of the Force. Tionne's students maintained their concentration.

The Dark Jedi swallowed hard.

"You can try to escape if you like," Tionne said. "Maybe you have enough power to subdue all of us with enough left over to catch that block of stone before it falls down on your heads. Maybe." She shrugged. "It's your choice, of course. But I wouldn't risk it."

The four Dark Jedi exchanged glances, unable to find words. Finally, one by one, they lowered their clenched hands and surrendered.

Tionne heaved a quiet but heartfelt sigh of relief.

Another tree stood in the forest, short and stunted, with a thick trunk. Branches extended out in such a way that, if looked at in a certain light, it had an almost humanoid appearance: one of Master Skywalker's Jedi, a slow-moving, long-lived plantlike creature.

She often went out to spend days in the sunlight, using photosynthesis to drink in nourishment, absorbing minerals from the soil, water from the river, and carbon dioxide from the air.

She would spend all day, many days at a time, simply contemplating the Force and her place in the universe. Trees remained alive for a long time and did not rush into ill-considered action; yet at times such as this, she could manage to move fast enough. She understood the importance of protecting the Jedi academy.

She had entered into her training to understand the Force, vowing to defend the side of light—and here she found herself in a clear-cut battle against the Shadow Academy. Dark Jedi enemies coursed through the jungle, searching for victims, but Master Skywalker had taught all the trainees well. The light-side students would put up a good fight.

The treelike Jedi stood motionless, watching, sensing the jungle . . . and she knew her enemies would come to her. She had only to wait. Her roots dug deeper into the soil, drawing on it for greater energy. She felt the sap pulsing through her, boiling in her veins, allowing her to gain the speed for the unwavering action that she would require just this once . . . she hoped.

She had chosen her spot well, next to an ailing Massassi tree, tall with outspreading branches. Its trunk was nested with vines and dripping with parasitic shelf mushrooms that had tapped into its heartwood and begun devouring the great tree from within.

The Jedi could tell that this great-grandfather of a tree had lived for centuries and centuries. . . . It was the way of things, the cycle of the forest. As plants grew, they went to seed to bear their young, and then slowly decayed to warm organic matter and fertilized the forest for subsequent generations. She saw how the old Massassi tree leaned, observed the surrounding jungle . . . waited.

She reached out with the Force subtly, gently, so that even the adepts of the Dark Side would not know they were being manipulated. *"Come here,"* she thought, broadcasting it over and over again. At least one of them would catch the hint. They would think they had detected one of their lightside enemies—but it would be all the plant Jedi's doing.

After an indeterminate period—she did not measure time in small increments—she sensed a clumsy disturbance: two attackers from the Shadow Academy storming through the forest, as if the delicate ecosystem was no more than a nuisance that they would eradicate completely, given the chance.

The Jedi waited. She had to concentrate. She had to act at the right moment and not waste time thinking, or else her opportunity would pass.

Curled within one of her gnarled branches— a handlike appendage—was a knobby lightsaber built to accommodate her wooden grip.

The two Dark Jedi came into the clearing and stopped. "I see nothing here," said one. "Lord Brakiss would be ashamed of you. Lord Zekk would take away your lightsaber. The powers of the dark side are wasted on you."

"I tell you, I sensed it," said the other. He stepped forward, looking from side to side, studying the quiet jungle. His companion stood next to him, scowling.

At that moment the Jedi used all her stored reserves—and acted. She ignited the lightsaber and slashed sideways with her branch arm, like a bent sapling suddenly released to snap straight again.

"I am sorry, Grandfather Tree," she said—and her lightsaber blade cleaved through the trunk of the tottering old Massassi tree, severing it from the stump and letting the arms of gravity embrace it. Its wide-branched top leaned over and the tree crashed onto the two Dark Jedi intruders. They had time only to look up with a muffled outcry of surprise as a meteor of branches and vines smashed down upon them.

The Jedi deactivated her lightsaber, then felt a trembling through her entire wooden body. In one act, she had drained months and months of her energy reserves. She stretched her branches up toward the sunlight, dug her roots deeper.

It would take her a long time to recover from this day.

9

AFTER CROSSING THE river, Jaina fought her way through the jungle, seeking a suitable path through the thickest underbrush while keeping herself hidden from other attackers. Right now, the tangled forest was her ally, and she could use the cover to her advantage. She wasn't afraid to combat the Dark Jedi threatening the academy—but she had a vital mission in mind . . . something more to her tastes.

As long as the defensive energy shields remained down and the generator damaged, the entire area was vulnerable to repeated attacks from the skies. Luke Skywalker's trainees were defending themselves . . . but if Jaina could somehow repair the shield generator and get the protective force field up again, the new Jedi Knights could take care of these audacious enemies one at a time.

Jaina finally made her way to the clearing where her father and Chewbacca had recently installed the new energy shield generator. With only a glance she saw that the machinery was irreparable, despite her usual knack for fixing things.

Normally, she could make temporary repairs to get systems up and running again, at least for a while. But not in this case. An Imperial saboteur had used thermal detonators to wipe out the entire generating station. It was hopelessly ruined, a pile of shrapnel; no simple fixup would do.

Jaina's attention remained on the generator for only a moment, however. She caught her breath.

There in the clearing sat an Imperial TIE fighter in perfect condition.

Ever since Chewbacca had given Lowie the T-23 skyhopper, Jaina had longed for a vehicle of her own. That, in fact, had been the impetus behind her desire to repair the crashed TIE fighter the young Jedi Knights had found in the jungles—Qorl's TIE fighter.

She stopped and stared, frozen with excitement and apprehension. But other than the muffled noises of battle in the jungles and the distant shouts and blaster fire near the Great Temple, she heard no sound.

Jaina withdrew her lightsaber and pressed the power stud. The beam sprang outward, glowing an electric violet. Then she crept forward stealthily, ready to fight if the TIE pilot emerged with his blaster drawn. But she sensed no one else around, heard no noise from the craft.

"Hello?" Jaina called. "You'd better surrender if you're an Imperial!" She waited. "Uh, is anyone here?"

Only the simmering jungle noises answered her.

Moving forward, letting her eagerness take over, she ran to the abandoned TIE fighter. It was a sinister-looking ship: a rounded cockpit suspended between two flat hexagonal power arrays, twin ion engines that would propel the small fighter across space, a bank of deadly laser cannons.

Ideas and possibilities thundered through her mind. If she could pilot this ship into the enemy's midst, Jaina would be in disguise. She could slip in among them, and they wouldn't *know* she was actually an enemy . . . until it was too late.

Switching off her lightsaber again, Jaina opened the cockpit hatch and crawled inside. She had studied how TIE fighters worked when she and her friends had replaced the components of Qorl's crashed ship. She knew the buttons on the control panels, knew how the systems activated. Though the exiled old pilot had flown off in his ship before Jaina had had a chance to take it on a flight, she was confident she could handle the craft.

She settled into the pilot's seat, noting the oily scent of stale lubricants and the sour odors the Empire did not bother to remove. A rebreather mask hung next to a small life-support console. The cockpit walls closed around her like a protective shell, giving her little room to move, but all the controls were at her fingertips. Through the ship's front ports, she could see outside.

Jaina found the power switch and toggled it on, felt the engines' thrumming, systems gearing up, batteries charging. Control panel lights winked on in a brilliant flurry around her. She drew a deep breath, strapped herself in, and clutched the controls.

"All systems ready for takeoff," she whispered to herself. She glanced at the sky, looking for the black specks of other Imperial ships. "Okay, TIE fighters, prepare for some company!"

The Imperial craft raised up as Jaina worked the controls. Clearing the jungle treetops, she felt the exhilaration of actually flying. The ship seemed unbelievably quiet inside, until she realized that its noisier primary engines had been disengaged. This TIE fighter flew so quietly because it used only the lesser-powered engines. So *that* was how the enemy pilot had gotten under their shield unnoticed! No doubt the original systems remained intact, but the enemy commando had slipped in without the familiar howl of TIE engines.

All right then, Jaina thought—she could be silent and deadly as well. Finally skimming the treetops, she scanned around, acquiring targets. She shot forward, reveling in the thrill of flight, the landscape passing beneath her in a mottled green blur.

Up ahead she saw six TIE fighters flying in formation, firing down at the treetops, pounding the temple ruins, even structures that had never been used for training Jedi. The Palace of the Woolamander, an ancient ruin already nearly collapsed, was pummeled with brilliant streaks from laser cannons, though Jaina didn't believe any Jedi Knights had gone there.

She kept the Imperial comm channels on so she could hear the terse, gruff chatter as the TIE pilots discussed their overall plan, choosing targets, firing at moving figures sheltered by the thick Massassi trees.

Jaina kept her microphone off, though, as

she joined the formation of TIE fighters, slipping in at the rear. Over the comm system she heard them acknowledge her arrival; rather than making them suspicious by speaking with a young woman's voice, she just clicked an okay over the microphone.

Then she powered up her laser cannons.

One of the TIE fighters broadcast, "Plenty of targets here for everybody. Let's cause some damage."

Jaina bit her lower lip and nodded. "Yes," she muttered to herself, "let's cause some damage."

She let her eyes fall partially closed and concentrated, feeling the Force. Despite the sensors and systems available in the TIE fighter, nothing could match heightened Jedi perceptions for enhancing her movements. She needed to target and fire and target again with lightning speed. She would have only one chance.

Jaina gripped the control stick of her weapons and focused on the aiming mechanisms, flying smoothly behind the unsuspecting Imperials. She had to disable them with one shot each. She couldn't risk repeated fire on a single target, because once she started shooting, they would be rather upset with her.

Jaina sought out the most vulnerable points: their engines and the joints that held the planar power arrays to their sides. If the TIE fighters turned side-on to her, she would blast the power arrays themselves—large targets, impossible to miss.

Giving herself a silent countdown, Jaina pointed her lasers at the closest ship. What am I waiting for? she asked herself.

Gritting her teeth, she fired a single shot, then swiveled the laser cannons, moving with hyperspeed, to target a second TIE fighter. Even before her second bolt struck the narrow joint next to the cockpit and sliced off the planar array, the first TIE fighter careened into a spin.

Jaina blasted again at the rear engine pods of the second ship. The TIE fighter exploded in front of her, momentarily blinding her, but she quickly averted her eyes. As she brought the laser cannons to bear on a third target, Jaina heard the TIE pilots shouting in outrage and panic. The formation began to split apart.

She didn't have much time.

The third TIE fighter turned toward her, and Jaina strafed across its surface, severing one of the planar arrays and striking the viewports in the cockpit. The third ship went down—but by now the remaining three Imperials had spun around and were headed straight toward her.

Jaina blinked as fiery bolts from their laser cannons shot past her. She put her TIE fighter into a spin. Now using the Force to anticipate the incoming weapons fire, just as her uncle Luke had used his lightsaber to deflect blaster bolts, she spun and turned and banked, then began to fly away at her fighter's top speed.

But the other three Imperial ships came howling after her, releasing a constant volley of laser fire, ignoring targets below now that they had acquired a single target . . . a traitor in their midst.

Jaina ducked and dodged, no longer enjoying the thrill of flight. She had a bad feeling about her impulsive attack. She streaked over the jungle, the three TIE fighters hot on her tail.

10

THE DIM FOREST floor near the Great Temple was familiar ground for Luke Skywalker and most of his Jedi trainees. Even with a battle of light and dark raging around him—or perhaps *because* of the battle—he found it soothing to be out in the wilds. The jungle itself was rich with life, and therefore rich in the Force that bound all life together.

Reaching down to confirm that his lightsaber was securely attached to his belt next to his comlink, Luke drew on the Force. He let it flow through him, let it show him the skirmishes all around him.

Alert to the emotions of his students, Luke reached out to bolster flagging confidence in one trainee, to warn another against an unexpected attack, to send encouragement to yet another who was growing tired.

An energy bolt from a TIE fighter sliced through the trees close by and set fire to the underbrush, forcing Luke to retreat behind a thicket to avoid choking fumes from the burning vegetation.

With his mind he searched for the center of the battle, the place where he could do the most good. Decades ago, when the Death Star had loomed over the jungle moon, his mission had been clear. The battle station's superlaser could turn an entire planet to rubble. Luke had had no doubt in his mind that the Empire's most powerful weapon must be destroyed. And with the Force to guide him, he had succeeded.

But today's battle was different—it had no focus. This time he had no superweapon to disable. The Jedi academy's long-range transmissions had been jammed, the defensive shields sabotaged. With Artoo-Detoo and the *Shadow Chaser* trapped in the Great Temple's hangar bay, Luke had no way of reaching orbit to fight the Shadow Academy directly.

The ground assault itself was directed from the giant battle platform that hovered over the treetops a few kilometers away, but Luke sensed that the military component of the attack was mere harassment.

TIE fighters had made direct attacks on the Great Temple—and yet *ground* forces and Dark Jedi had been sent to fight on a nearly even footing against Luke's students. With a different strategy, the Shadow Academy's victory would have been far easier—it almost seemed as if Brakiss *wanted* to do it the hard way.

Luke knew that must be the answer.

A loud incoming message signal on his comlink startled him. Students at the Yavin academy rarely carried comlinks, but the Jedi Master kept one at his side during times of turmoil so that he could be reached more easily. Even though the Shadow Academy had jammed long-range transmissions, local signals from Artoo could still get through.

Luke switched on the comlink. "Sit tight, Artoo. We'll be able to get you when the fighting's over." Before he could say more, a man's voice blared from the tiny speaker.

"—essage for Luke Skywalker. Repeat: this is a message for Luke Skywalker. If anyone can hear me, respond immediately."

Luke stared at the small device before replying, "Who is this?" But before he heard the answer, his Jedi senses told him the man's identity.

"You can call me *Master* Brakiss," the voice said. "Tell your teacher that I'm transmitting on all channels. He will want to speak to me."

"This is Luke Skywalker," he said. "If you have a message, Brakiss, you can give it directly to me." Luke's heart knocked painfully against his rib cage, though from surprise rather than fear.

A cultured laugh came over the comlink. "Well, my old teacher . . . the man I once called Master. This *is* a pleasure."

"What do you want, Brakiss?" Luke asked.

"A meeting," the smooth voice replied. "Just the two of us. On neutral ground. As equals. We didn't have a chance to finish our . . . conversation when you came to my Shadow Academy to rescue your Jedi brats."

Luke paused to consider. A meeting with Brakiss? Maybe this was the answer to the problem he had been trying to solve. After all, who was more central to this battle than the leader of the Shadow Academy himself? If Luke could reason with Brakiss, turn him away from the dark side, this battle could be won before too many lives were lost.

"Where, Brakiss? What neutral territory do you propose?"

"I think both your academy and mine are out of the question right now."

"Agreed."

"Away from the fighting, then. Across the

river in the Temple of the Blue Leaf Cluster. But you must come alone."

"Will *you*?" Luke asked.

Brakiss gave a rich chuckle. "Of course. I have no need for reinforcements—and I know you are true to your word."

Luke paused to reassure himself that the Force was indeed guiding his actions. Both he and Brakiss were strong enough in the Force to sense any betrayal by the other.

"Very well, Brakiss. I'll meet you there. Alone. We can settle this once and for all."

11

"HEY, THAT WASN'T so hard," Jacen said, leaning forward in the copilot's chair of the *Lightning Rod*. The chair creaked, its padding bulging out through countless small rips and tears in the cushion. The engines rumbled and coughed and whined as the cargo shuttle finally broke free of the atmosphere.

"You had to say that, didn't you, boy?" Peckhum said as sensor alarms squealed on his control panel. Incoming enemy ships. Again. "We got TIE fighters coming, four of 'em. Looks like they were launched directly from the Shadow Academy."

Jacen swallowed, studying the pattern, and shook his head. "Oh, blaster bolts! We'd better transmit our distress message now before they get us. Otherwise help for the Jedi academy will come too late."

Peckhum looked over at him, his eyes red-rimmed, his haggard face serious.

"You'll have to take care of that message yourself, Jacen. I'm gonna be mighty busy doing some fancy flying here—if she'll hold together." He patted the cockpit controls. "Sorry to do this to you, girl, but I didn't name you the *Lightning Rod* for nothing. Let's show these Imperials our stuff."

Jacen fumbled with the unfamiliar comm system, tuning frequencies and feeling completely inadequate. He wished his sister were here—*she* was the expert on these systems. She would know how to cut through the double-talk, the chatter, the Imperial transmission block.

He sent a subspace message blaring on all frequencies at the maximum levels of volume and power the *Lightning Rod* could spare and still keep her shields up.

"This is Jacen Solo," he said, then cleared his throat. He had no idea what to say, but he supposed the details didn't exactly matter. "Attention, New Republic. We have an emergency! This is Jacen Solo on Yavin 4, requesting immediate assistance. We are under attack by the Shadow Academy!

"Repeat. Imperial fighters attacking the Jedi academy—request assistance immediately. Our shields are down. We've got ground battles taking place and air strikes from TIE fighters. We desperately need immediate assistance." He switched off the microphone, then looked over at Peckhum. "Hey, how'd I do?"

"Just fine, kid," Peckhum said, and lurched the ship to one side, going into a clockwise spin as the four TIE fighters roared past, belching fire from laser cannons. One shot struck the *Lightning Rod*'s lower shield, but the other bolts streamed harmlessly into space, intersecting the empty void where the cargo ship had been only a moment before.

"I used to be a pretty good flier in my day," Peckhum said. "And I still am . . . I think."

One TIE fighter broke away from the other three and spun in a tighter circle, firing repeatedly without taking the trouble to aim, spraying space with its deadly fire.

Peckhum dove down, skimming the atmosphere, so that the lower hull of the *Lightning Rod* grew hot. Then he bounced back into space again, turning about in a tight backward loop and heading up over the determined TIE fighter, which shot again and again. Sparks flew from the battered supply ship's control panels. Lights winked red on their system diagnostics.

"Uh, Peckhum? What do all those alarms mean?" Jacen said.

"It means our shields are failing."

"Don't you have any *weapons* on this ship?" Jacen scanned the panels, looking for any sort of targeting system, some firing controls.

Peckhum coughed and put the ship into a sharp dive toward Yavin 4. "This is a cargo ship, boy, and she's seen better days. I wasn't expecting to take her into battle, you know. Heck, I'm lucky the food-prep units still work."

The rest of the Imperial squadron zoomed away to continue the attack on the Jedi academy, but the one persistent TIE fighter came in again single-mindedly. This time he had them locked on target, so that most of his laser cannon blasts struck the *Lightning Rod*.

"This guy really wants to take us out," Jacen said.

Peckhum pushed his accelerators well beyond maximum safety levels. The *Lightning Rod* groaned and creaked as it rattled down through the atmosphere, buffeted by air turbulence.

Jacen was thrown from side to side. He grabbed the comm system again. "This is Jacen Solo with a personal distress this time.

We are in deep trouble. Someone is on our tail. Request assistance. Please—can anyone out there help us?"

Peckhum looked over at him. "Nobody's going to get here in time."

Jacen remembered stories of how Luke Skywalker had been in a similar situation on the run down the Death Star trench, trying to send his proton torpedo through a small thermal exhaust port. His X-wing had been in Darth Vader's sights, unable to shake the TIE fighters and interceptors on his tail. Things had looked hopeless—and then Jacen's father, Han Solo, had appeared out of nowhere, saving the day.

But Jacen didn't think his father was anywhere close by now, and he couldn't imagine anyone else who might pop unexpectedly out of the skies to take care of the enemy. That was too much luck to hope for.

With a crackle of static over the comm system, a gruff and gloating voice spoke—but it wasn't any rescuer. "Well . . . Jacen Solo! You're one of those feisty Jedi brats we ran into down in the lower levels of Coruscant. Remember me—Norys? I was the leader of the Lost Ones gang. You stole that hawk-bat egg from us . . . and now I think we're about to even all the old scores. Hah!"

Jacen felt a shiver go down his spine as he remembered the broad-shouldered bully who had such an appetite for destruction. Norys continued.

"The little trash collector, Zekk, joined us in the Second Imperium, but *you* have made the wrong choice, boy. I just wanted you to know who was going to blast you to slag." The TIE pilot signed off and continued the conversation with a volley of laser bolts.

"Well, I'm glad he picked such a fine time to contact us," Peckhum said, fighting with the controls, unable to fly an evasive pattern anymore. He worked with all his talent just to keep the *Lightning Rod* from falling apart in the sky. "I don't think we'll last much longer, and I'm sure that Norys kid would have hated to blow us up before he got a chance to say his little goodbye."

The engines of the *Lightning Rod* began to smoke. More alarms blared from the control panels. Behind them Norys's TIE fighter continued to fire mercilessly, pounding their hull, trying to crack open the battered cargo ship.

Jacen stared at the comm unit, but didn't think it would do any good to send out another distress signal.

The jungle treetops rushed by beneath

them. Jacen looked wildly from side to side. "I don't suppose it would be a good time to tell a joke," he said.

Peckhum shook his head. "Don't feel much like laughing right now."

12

THE THICK BRANCHES of the damp and shadowy jungle closed around him, pressing in. It reminded Zekk of the murky lower levels of Coruscant. It felt almost like home.

He and his troops of Dark Jedi had fallen from the skies, buoyed by repulsorpacks. After coming to rest in the upper branches, they'd worked their way down to ground level and spread out to surround the fleeing Jedi trainees Master Skywalker had brainwashed into supporting Rebel philosophies.

Zekk knew little about politics. He understood only who his friends and supporters were—and who had betrayed him. Like Jacen and Jaina . . . especially Jaina. He had thought she was his friend, a close companion. Only later, after Brakiss had explained it, did Zekk understand what Jaina really thought of him, how easily she dismissed his Jedi potential and the possibility that he might be an equal to her and her high-born twin brother. But Zekk *did* have the potential, and he had proved it.

In spite of this, he hoped Jacen and Jaina would not fight him, because then he would have to demonstrate his power—and his loyalty to the Second Imperium. He remembered his first test against Tamith Kai's prize student Vilas, and Vilas had paid with his life.

In the upper branches of a tree overhead, one Dark Jedi fighter had become tangled. Zekk watched as the bright arc of a lightsaber blade slashed boughs out of the way, clearing a path for the fighter to descend to the lower levels.

Overhead a wing of TIE fighters roared across the skies, firing into the forest. The Dark Jedi spread out, looking for potential victims on their own. Zekk gathered three of the nearest fighters to his side and they marched along, crashing through the underbrush.

They reached the edge of the wide river, whose brown-green currents lapped quietly through the jungle, stirring overhanging fronds. Farther downstream, closer to the tall Massassi temple ruins, he saw Tamith Kai's hovering battle platform.

Zekk stood beside his Dark Jedi companions on the riverbank. The other fighters exchanged glances and pointed skyward. Zekk nodded, knowing what they wished to do. "Yes," he said. "Let us conjure a storm, a great wind to knock the jungle flat and send these Jedi cowards scurrying."

He looked up into the clear blue skies and reached deep within his heart, finding a shadow of anger, the pain he had felt in his life. He knew how to use anger as a tool, a weapon. Zekk gathered the winds. Beside him, he felt the other dark-side warriors doing the same, drawing thunderheads until lumpy black clouds rolled in from the horizon.

The wind picked up and grew colder, charged with static electricity. Zekk's scarlet-lined cape rippled around him. Stray strands of his dark hair whipped around his face as the wind snatched them free of his ponytail. Flashing bolts of lightning skittered from one thunderhead to another. The rumble of noise drowned out even the sound of TIE fighters crisscrossing overhead.

Zekk smiled. Yes, a storm was coming, a victorious storm.

But as the clouds continued to swell, releasing a powerful weather energy, he heard sounds of repeated laser cannon fire and glanced to the sky, where another battle was taking place: a one-sided dogfight. A smoking ship careened overhead, pursued by a lone TIE fighter that shot its energy bolts again and again, mercilessly pummeling its prey.

Astonished, Zekk recognized the clunky patchwork form of the *Lightning Rod*, the cargo ship of his old friend Peckhum, the man with whom he had lived for many years.

Peckhum! They had been close companions, good friends despite how little they had in common. Too late, he remembered that the old spacer earned extra credits by making occasional supply runs to Skywalker's Jedi academy. Could it be that his old friend had been here on the jungle moon when this morning's attack began?

His heart sank, and a wrenching dismay filled his stomach. His concentration on the storm faltered.

In the backlash, winds whipped the trees closer to him, blowing back branches as the other Dark Jedi struggled to retain control of the gusting squall.

"No, Peckhum," Zekk said, looking up as he watched the TIE fighter blasting the hapless *Lightning Rod*. A small explosion flared on its hull, and Zekk knew that the battered supply ship had just lost its shields.

The *Lightning Rod* was going down—and there was nothing he could do about it.

He heard shouts of surprise next to him as the Dark Jedi Knights completely lost control of the gathering storm. The winds continued to snap branches and uproot saplings, then gradually dissipated as the dark-side warriors stopped manipulating the weather.

Their attention had been drawn to a young Jedi trainee they discovered in the underbrush—someone who had either been creeping up on them or simply hiding from Zekk's advance.

The boy scrambled out of the weeds, spiky pale hair blowing around his flushed face. His clothes and robes were so ridiculously garish—bright purples and golds and greens and reds—that they hurt Zekk's eyes. How could this young man have thought to hide while dressed like that?

The boy appeared frightened, but determined. He thrust his lower lip out and stood with his hands on his hips, his rainbow-colored robes rippling around him in the last vestiges of the angry wind.

"Very well, you give me no choice," the boy said, then cleared his throat. "I am Raynar, Jedi Knight . . . uh, in training. You will either surrender now—or force me to attack you."

Two of Zekk's companions laughed in wholehearted amusement, ignited their lightsabers, and stalked toward the trapped young man. Raynar stepped backward until he bumped against the rough trunk of a tree. He squeezed his eyes shut, struggling to concentrate. He held his breath until his face turned bright red, then purplish.

Zekk felt a slight invisible push as the boy attempted to use the Force to drive them back. The two lightsaber-bearing Dark Jedi seemed not even to notice.

Zekk found, though, that he had no stomach for outright slaughter. This boy seemed proud and brash, but there was something about him—an innocence . . .

Thinking quickly, before his two companions could drive in and make short work of Raynar, Zekk reached out with the Force, grabbed the boy by his bright robes, and yanked him off his feet. With a flick of his mind, he hurled Raynar over the heads of his companions, tossing him out into the river. Raynar yowled as he flew, then plunged belly-first into the thin, muddy waters.

The two Dark Jedi whirled, looking angrily at Zekk. Out in the water, Raynar splashed to the shallows, completely soaked in mud, his robes covered with river slime.

"It is a greater victory to utterly humiliate your enemy than simply to kill him," Zekk said. "And we have humiliated this Jedi in a way he will never forget."

The dark warriors next to him chuckled at the observation, and Zekk knew he had defused their anger . . . for the moment, at least.

Then he looked longingly into the sky, hoping to spot any trace of the *Lightning Rod*, but he saw only a dissipating cloud of smoke overhead. He wished he could find some way to help his friend; would he be forced to count the loss of Peckhum as part of the cost of victory?

The wounded ship had passed out of sight to where the battle would reach its foregone conclusion. He was certain he would never see the *Lightning Rod* or Peckhum again.

13

QORL'S TIE FIGHTER flew low over the jungle, mapping out targets for the assault squadron. The rest of his fighter wing had their own orders, and they flew in their own attack patterns.

He doubted, though, that his student Norys would bother to follow orders once the battles actually started and laser shots began to fly. The bully would blunder from target to target like a mad gundark, likely to cause as much damage to the Imperial plans as he did to the Rebels.

Qorl felt cold inside, liquid dismay hardening to ice. He had expected to be exhilarated by flying and fighting again, piloting his own TIE fighter in battle for the Second Imperium.

Instead, he had only reservations and second thoughts. He dreaded the possibility that he had made a bad decision and that the

Second Imperium might have to pay the price.

Norys continued to be a great disappointment. When Qorl had selected the tough young man, he knew the bully's personality had hardened during years of harsh living, though he had lorded over the Lost Ones on Coruscant. The broad-shouldered boy had been dedicated, vowing to become an Imperial soldier because it gave him a feeling of power and confidence—exactly what the Second Imperium needed.

However, a loyal soldier was also required to obey orders. A servant of the Empire couldn't be a loose cannon, following his own wishes rather than the commands of his superiors. As he'd grown accustomed to his situation, Norys had become increasingly disrespectful, even insubordinate.

The bully was truly bloodthirsty, wanting simply to dominate, to cause pain, to achieve utter victory. He did not fight for the glory of the Second Imperium, or for bringing back the New Order—or for any sort of political goal. He fought simply to *fight*. And that was a deadly attitude, no matter which side he fought for.

Qorl circled, zeroing in on a raging forest fire that had been started by one of the TIE bombers, then streaked along the river to where Tamith Kai's battle platform hovered over the trees. Over his cockpit communication channel, Qorl heard a loud, desperate transmission on all bands—and recognized the voice.

"Attention, New Republic. We have an emergency! This is Jacen Solo on Yavin 4, requesting immediate assistance. We are under attack by the Shadow Academy!"

Qorl sat up, adjusted his black helmet, and flew steadily. He remembered the young twins who had helped fix his TIE fighter, the brother and sister who had been his prisoners around the campfire in the depths of the jungle. They had offered him friendship . . . and tried to turn him from his loyalty to the Second Imperium. But he had been indoctrinated too well.

Surrender is betrayal.

So Qorl had escaped and made his way to the Shadow Academy, where he had watched as the twins were brought in to be trained under the murderous tutelage of Tamith Kai and Brakiss. Qorl had been deeply disturbed by the violence of their instruction, the disregard for the lives of the fresh students.

No one had ever found out that Qorl had

discreetly assisted the young friends in their escape as they fled the Shadow Academy. After that Qorl had privately done everything he could to atone for the indiscretion, making his raid on the Rebel convoy to steal hyper-drive cores and turbolaser batteries, then working hard to train Norys and the other new stormtroopers.

A smoking ship streaked overhead: a blaster-scarred and battered cargo trans-port. Qorl recognized the model of the ship, an unarmed carrier vessel of an old design. Its engines were sluggish, its shields not designed or reinforced for combat.

And now he saw that it was being pur-sued by a relentless TIE fighter.

Qorl was ashamed to see the TIE pilot waste shot after shot, although sheer luck allowed some of the laser bolts to strike the hull. It would be only a matter of time before the cargo ship exploded in midair.

Qorl tuned his cockpit comm systems to a direct channel with the other TIE fighter. "TIE pilot, identify yourself."

The gruff voice that responded came as no surprise to Qorl. "This is Norys, old man. Don't bother me—I've got a target in my sights."

He swallowed, but his throat remained dry. "Norys, you have already crippled the target. That cargo ship is not our main objective. Your orders are to disable the Jedi academy. That ship won't be causing any more trouble for the Second Imperium."

"Leave off, old man," Norys said. "This is *my* kill, and I'm gonna score it."

Qorl tried to keep his anger in check. "We don't keep score, Norys. This assault is for the Second Imperium—not for your personal glory."

"Go stick your head up an exhaust tube," Norys said. "I'm not letting an old coward tell me what to do." Then the bully switched off his comm system and plunged after the burning cargo ship, firing with absolute abandon.

Qorl's disappointment turned to outrage. This young man's attitude flew in the face of everything admirable about the Empire. Qorl remembered his earlier TIE fighter training, how he and his fellow pilots had all worked together like a machine: precise, well mannered, respectful, listening to orders—promoting the orderly lifestyle the Emperor had brought to the galaxy. *That* was worth fighting for.

But Norys did not represent such a philosophy. He didn't care.

The broadband comm signal came across his speakers again. "This is Jacen Solo with a personal distress this time. We are in deep trouble. Someone is on our tail. Request assistance. Please—can anyone out there help us?"

Qorl flew beneath the aerial dogfight just above the treetops, anguished inside. Jacen Solo was an honorable opponent. The boy had a strong heart, though he had fallen in with the Rebel band instead of the Second Imperium. But could the boy be blamed? After all, his mother was the Chief of State of the Rebel government.

Norys, however, *did* have a choice. The broad-shouldered boy knew what he had been trained for. He had adopted his Imperial uniform and his ship willingly . . . yet now he refused to play by the rules. Norys was no better than a ruthless, murderous bully.

The pursuing TIE fighter continued to fly in the slipstream of the crippled cargo vessel. Black smoke curled up from her engine pods, and Qorl observed the precise moment at which the shields failed.

Norys fired again, staining the hull with a slash of black blisters.

Qorl flicked on his own laser cannons and activated the targeting systems. The *Lightning Rod* would explode in a matter of seconds under Norys's continued assault. If it did, Qorl wouldn't be surprised if the bully continued to shoot the burning wreckage to make sure there were no survivors.

Disgust welled up within him. Switching off his comm system, he muttered, "Do I lose any honor by destroying someone who has no honor of his own?"

Qorl had studied every subsystem on the Imperial TIE fighters. He knew their weak points. Qorl knew how to destroy them.

He targeted Norys's reactor exhausts.

Ignoring his teacher entirely, Norys fired again. His lasers had fallen into a slower repeating rhythm now, as if he savored these last few moments.

The *Lightning Rod* lurched, in one last helpless attempt to dodge the laser fire.

Qorl closed in on Norys's ship.

And fired.

Norys's TIE fighter exploded in the air, annihilated so quickly and completely that the young bully didn't even have time to cry out in surprise.

Ashamed that his act had been a betrayal of the Second Imperium, Qorl made no attempt to contact the *Lightning Rod*. He simply changed course and swerved back toward the main battlefield, while the faltering *Lightning Rod* struggled to remain aloft . . . or at least to land without crashing too badly.

14

WHILE BATTLES RAGED above the Jedi academy and in the jungle around it, Imperial commando Orvak crept forward, intent on his mission.

He had left his TIE fighter behind in the wake of the explosions at the shield generator facility, but he would come back to it once he had finished here. For hours now, he had made his way secretly through the thick forest.

Several trees burned in the jungle nearby, sending up coils of putrid smoke from the wet vegetation. He heard blaster fire and shouts, the distant hum of lightsabers. He kept low and quiet, not willing to risk giving away his position.

Skywalker's Jedi had abandoned their Great Temple to engage in scattered skirmishes in the forests . . . leaving it open and unprotected for him to do his work.

Approaching the ancient edifice, still

hidden by the jungle, Orvak saw black streaks on the thick stone—blaster scoring and scars from proton explosives dropped by TIE bombers. The ubiquitous vines that clung to the pyramid's sides had withered under the fire and fallen away in heaps. One close explosion had wrecked the temple's hangar bay door, preventing Skywalker's fleet of guardian ships from launching.

So, Orvak thought, after all these millennia, this ancient structure had finally been damaged. But it wasn't damaged enough. He would take care of the rest.

Moving carefully, ducking his helmeted head, he crept through the foliage, ripping up vines and uprooting ferns to clear the way until he finally emerged from the underbrush and stood behind the tall temple.

Above, TIE fighters streaked like birds of prey across the sky; Orvak looked up, silently urging them on.

To one side of the pyramid he saw a newly laid flagstone courtyard. Across it, at the base of the stone structure, a darkened entrance stood open. Imagining what sort of fearful sorcerous exercises the Jedi students performed there, he stepped cautiously into the courtyard.

Already weeds had begun to push up between the flagstones. The jungle would no doubt reclaim its own within a matter of months after he destroyed the temple—and it would be good riddance to this place, he thought. By then he hoped either to be back on the Shadow Academy or perhaps promoted to officer rank on a Star Destroyer . . . if his mission today turned out well enough.

When the fighting became particularly loud, and proton bombs exploded in the jungle not far away, Orvak made his move. He rushed across the heavy flagstones to the dim doorway that led into the Rebels' secret temple.

He paused at the threshold for a moment, glad for his helmet in case poisonous vapors might seep out from the interior. Who knew what booby traps the Jedi sorcerers might have laid?

He used the sensors in his helmet to check for traps, but found none . . . which wasn't surprising, since the Shadow Academy's attack had been completely unexpected; the Jedi Knights had not had time to prepare.

Orvak entered the Massassi temple, shouldering his pack. He raced down the corridors, unfamiliar with the layout of the pyramid. He saw living quarters, large dining halls . . . nothing of significance that he could destroy.

He made his way down to the rubble-sealed hangar bay, where he thought he could plant his detonators to best effect and blow up all the Rebel starfighters. But when he emerged from the turbolift, he squinted in the dim lighting, unable to believe what he saw. Orvak found only a single, sleek-looking ship, all curves and angles. Nothing more. No fleet of spacecraft, no major defenses. He snorted in disbelief.

Suddenly, alarms squealed out from the hangar bay. Flashing red lights stabbed at his eyes. A small barrel-shaped droid hurtled toward him, whistling and screeching. Blue electric bolts sparked from a welding arm that protruded from its cylindrical torso.

Orvak slammed himself back into the turbolift, punching the controls to seal the doors. Could the Jedi have installed a force of assassin droids? Lethal, weapon-wielding machines that would never, *ever* miss?

But as the doors sealed shut and the turbolift whisked him upward, his last glimpse showed him that the attacker was simply a lone astromech droid trundling across the floor, sounding the standard alarms installed in its base. Apparently, however, no one remained in the temple to hear them.

He chuckled nervously. One astromech droid! It annoyed him when mere machines held too great a sense of their own importance. He no longer feared a trap.

Orvak had to find a different place for his purposes anyway. Someplace more special.

He finally located it on the highest level of the great pyramid.

Taking the turbolift to the top, and holding his blaster ready to shoot anyone who came out of the shadows, the Imperial commando stepped into the grand audience chamber.

Here, the walls were polished and inlaid with multicolored stones. At one end rose a great stage, from which Orvak could imagine the Rebels gave lectures to their students, handed medals to each other after victories in the war against the rightful rulers of the galaxy, perhaps even performed their disgusting rituals.

Yes, he thought. *Perfect.*

Moving quickly, heart pounding with the thrill of accomplishing the mission that had already cost the life of his companion Dareb, Orvak unslung his pack. He pulled off his black helmet to see better in the light that filtered through the temple skylights.

Smoke blackened the sky outside, like burnt paint brushed across the air. Distant sounds of the continuing attack echoed like ricochets inside the audience chamber. But he heard no one else nearby, no movement. The temple was empty, and he had the time to work.

Orvak strode up to the stage, his boots thumping on the stone floor. Yes, that would be the best place, a central location where the incredible blast could reflect from all sides. He yanked off his heavy gloves so that he could tinker with the fine electronic components.

Working cautiously, he removed his seven remaining high-powered detonators and linked them together. Then, he plugged all of the explosives into a central countdown timer and spread them out like the spokes of a wheel in the grand audience chamber.

Yes, it would be a fine explosion.

Ideally, when all the detonators went off simultaneously, the explosion would rip off the top of the temple like a volcano erupting. The shock wave would punch through the floor to the levels below and blast the walls outward. The entire pyramid would come tumbling down, no more than a pile of ancient rubble—as it deserved to be.

Orvak returned to the central unit and fiddled with the controls, kneeling on the polished surface of the stage. He thought with smug satisfaction that no more Rebels would ever lecture here. No future Jedi Knights would learn Rebel ways. This room would hold no more victory celebrations.

Soon it would all be gone.

Kneeling on the ground, Orvak keyed in the initiating code. All around the chamber, detonator lights winked green, ready to go, waiting for him to send the final command. Surveying his handiwork, he smiled and pressed the ACTIVATE button. The timer began to count down. Not much time left for the Jedi academy.

As he moved, resting his hand on the floor, Orvak caught a glimmer of motion out of the corner of his eye . . . something glittering and translucent, almost transparent; it had caught a reflection of the light somehow.

He pulled out his blaster, remaining in a protective crouch. "Who's there?" he called.

Then he saw it again, an iridescent sinuous shape slithering toward him across the stage. He lost sight of it once more.

Orvak fired his blaster, gouging holes in the floor around him. Streaks of energy bolts ricocheted around him. He flattened himself on the stage, afraid of return fire. He couldn't see the shimmering invisible thing anymore, and wondered what it could have been. Some sorcerer's trick, no doubt. He shouldn't have dropped his guard, but the Jedi would never get him.

Just then, Orvak felt needles of pain sting his hand. He looked down to see tiny droplets of blood welling from two punctures in his palm—and the triangle head of some kind of viper, a glassy crystalline snake!

"Hey!" he shouted.

Before he could lash out at it, the crystal snake dropped away from him and slithered toward a narrow crack in the wall. Orvak saw a last spangle of light, and then the serpent disappeared. . . .

But by now he was beyond caring, because a warm fog of sleepiness had begun to steal over him. The pain from the snakebite in his hand dulled to a throb, and Orvak thought drowsily that a long sleep could only make it better.

He collapsed into a deep slumber right beside the countdown timer.

The numbers ticked inexorably downward.

15

TENEL KA STOOD at the edge of the Imperial battle platform, her muscles tense, her body and reflexes ready to react.

She coiled her fibercord before returning it and the grappling hook to her belt. Then, with her single muscular arm, she held up her rancor-tooth lightsaber and ignited it. Beside her towered Lowbacca, ginger fur standing on end, dark lips peeled back to reveal fangs. The Wookiee used both hands to grip his clublike lightsaber with its molten bronze blade.

Surprised to see unexpected enemies, stormtroopers on the battle platform marched forward with blasters drawn, confident of their victory.

Em Teedee wailed. "Oh dear, Master Lowbacca—perhaps we should have planned this attack a bit more thoroughly."

Lowie snarled, but Tenel Ka stood tall,

her confidence unshaken. "The Force is with us," she said. "This is a fact."

A single TIE bomber swooped overhead, dropping proton torpedoes into the forests. The sounds of blaster fire ricocheted around them.

On the raised command deck of the battle platform, the Nightsister Tamith Kai stood in her black cloak like a preening bird of prey. She turned, her midnight hair writhing around her head with static electricity, her wine-dark lips curled in a sneer. Tenel Ka and Lowie took three brave steps toward the waiting stormtroopers.

One of the white-armored soldiers, apparently nervous at seeing the two young Jedi Knights, fired his blaster—and Tenel Ka whipped her energy blade across to intersect the incoming energy bolt, deflecting it into the sky.

Then, by unspoken agreement, she and Lowie charged forward, yelling. They slashed with their lightsabers so furiously that though the stormtroopers sent out a volley of blaster fire, they were thrown into chaos. Lowie and Tenel Ka forced their way through them like a whirlwind.

On the command deck above, Tamith Kai strode forward to gaze down at the skirmish. "The girl is mine. I'll crush her heart myself," she said.

Tenel Ka slashed once more with her lightsaber, taking out another charging stormtrooper. She turned. Her heart thudded, but her breath came slow and even. Her muscles sang. She was prepared for this fight, sure of her physical abilities. This would be her best battle ever.

"That leaves all the other stormtroopers for you, Lowie," she said, springing up onto the command deck to meet her nemesis.

The young Wookiee roared his readiness, though Em Teedee did not sound quite as courageous. "Please be cautious, Master Lowbacca. It wouldn't be wise to get delusions of grandeur."

The stormtroopers pressed forward, fifteen against one gangly young Wookiee. Lowbacca didn't seem to think the odds were too bad.

Tenel Ka stood before the Nightsister, holding herself tall and proud, her turquoise lightsaber in front of her. She remembered the first time she had taken the evil woman by surprise and nearly crippled her. "So, how is your knee, Tamith Kai?"

The Nightsister's violet eyes flashed, and she shook her head mockingly. "Why not

surrender now, weakling girl?" she said.
"This is hardly a worthwhile test of my
abilities. Ha! A one-armed child who dares
to think she can be a threat to me."

"You talk too much," Tenel Ka said. "Or do
you intend to use your foul breath as a
weapon against me?"

"You have been around those twin Jedi
brats too long," Tamith Kai said. "You've
learned disrespect for your superiors." The
Nightsister jabbed the air with her fingers
and sent a bolt of blue-black lightning toward the warrior girl from Dathomir.

"I see no one here who is my superior,"
Tenel Ka said, intercepting the lightning
bolts with her lightsaber blade. Then she
used the Force to build her own positive
thoughts and feelings, which she pulled
around her like a shield. The Nightsister
retreated a step, taken aback.

Down one level, Lowbacca slashed with
his bronze lightsaber in one hand while
picking up a white-armored figure with his
other. He tossed the stormtrooper into three
other attackers, knocking them all down.
The Imperial soldiers were crowded too
closely together to use their blasters. They
seemed intent on taking down the angry

Wookiee through the sheer force of their own numbers.

It was a big mistake.

Up on the command deck the Nightsister circled, eyeing her young quarry with amusement. Tenel Ka held her lightsaber steady, locking her granite-gray eyes on the violet irises of her opponent.

Overhead, TIE bombers swooped down, though the pilots seemed more interested in the duel on the battle platform than in their bombing runs.

The Nightsister curled her hands, and a ball of blue lightning crackled in each palm, gathering strength. Tenel Ka knew she had to use the Nightsister's moment of concentration for a quick surprise.

Tamith Kai stood near the edge of the upper command deck as Lowie and the stormtroopers continued to battle one level below her. The Nightsister raised her hands. Evil fire crackled at her fingertips, waiting to be released.

Tenel Ka feinted with her lightsaber and then, completely without warning, used the Force to reach forward like an outstretched hand. She nudged the Nightsister, pushing her just enough that she stumbled over the edge. With a wild shriek, Tamith Kai toppled backward. Bolts of blue lightning sprayed harmlessly into the sky and barely missed a heavily armored TIE bomber that swooped overhead.

The Nightsister crashed among the stormtroopers and Lowbacca, who snarled at her. Stormtroopers rushed the Wookiee, trying to drag him down, but Tamith Kai blindly released her anger, blasting them all away from her.

From the command deck Tenel Ka looked up toward the loud sound of an approaching engine—and saw a TIE bomber cruising in low, targeting its laser cannons on *her*! Brilliant shots streaked out, melting holes in the deck plating at her feet.

The warrior girl danced from one side to the other, using her attunement with the Force to second-guess where the bolts would strike. The high-powered weapons were too strong for her to deflect with a mere lightsaber. She stood all alone, unprotected—an easy target.

Grimly, she made up her mind. As the Imperial fighter roared overhead, Tenel Ka locked her lightsaber blade on, then carefully estimated the proper trajectory. Underhanded, she hurled her rancor-tooth weapon up at the craft.

She had spent a great deal of time practicing her aim, throwing spears and knives, striking her chosen target every time. But here the timing was rushed and the distance greater. Still, she never doubted her ability.

The TIE bomber arched upward, gaining altitude as it curved around for a final attack run.

Her lightsaber cartwheeled through the air and, with a blazing turquoise flash, struck the side of the TIE bomber. It did not slice off one of the power-array panels as she had hoped. Instead, the energy blade sheared off a stabilizer device and ripped open a hole in the bomber's hull. Her lightsaber passed completely through, then plunged downward into the jungle thickness below near the edge of the river.

Unable to articulate words, the Nightsister lunged back onto the command deck with a yowl of vengeful rage. Her black cape flapped like the wings of a raven swooping in for the kill. Tamith Kai's eyes blazed with violet fury.

Seeing the one-armed girl standing all alone without so much as a lightsaber, the Nightsister began to laugh. Her deep, guttural chuckle was filled with derision. "And now you are dis*armed*," Tamith Kai sneered, looking at the stump of Tenel Ka's arm. "You waste my time, child. Why don't you save us both some trouble and just lie down and die?"

Tenel Ka glared at the Nightsister coldly and moved a step forward, showing no sign of hesitation. "I may be disarmed," she said, "but I am *never* without a weapon."

With that, her left foot flashed out, swept around, and caught Tamith Kai just behind her heel. At the same time, Tenel Ka slammed her palm into the center of the Nightsister's chest and pushed forward, toppling her opponent to the deck.

She heard the stormtroopers shouting in panic—then overhead came the rattling whine of a TIE bomber in trouble. Tenel Ka flicked her glance up, and reacted instantly.

The TIE bomber she had struck with her lightsaber had managed to circle back— although its rear compartment was now in flames. Entirely out of control, wobbling and careening from side to side, the desperate craft came toward the battle platform.

Tenel Ka could vaguely sense the pilot's terror. He didn't know what to do and saw the platform as his last chance, a place where he might make an emergency landing. But Tenel Ka could tell from the speed of his descent and his total lack of maneuverability that a landing was impossible.

Seeing nothing but her own rage, the Nightsister lunged with one clawed hand to grab Tenel Ka's ankle. The dark woman didn't even notice the approaching danger.

Tenel Ta could waste no time fighting with her. She snatched her booted foot free and leaped over the black-clad Nightsister, landing among the stormtroopers next to Lowie.

The stormtroopers, though, had already seen the incoming TIE bomber and scrambled to clear the deck.

"Lowbacca, we must go now," Tenel Ka said, grabbing his hairy arm.

He roared, and Em Teedee chimed in. "Indeed. I believe that is a most sensible suggestion."

She and Lowbacca hurried to the edge of the hovering platform and looked down at the sluggish river below and the overhanging jungle trees.

Up on the command deck, Tamith Kai finally realized the impending danger as the TIE bomber came in, its engines building to a sputtering roar. The Nightsister screamed for the pilots inside the battle platform to start its repulsor engines and evade the impending crash.

They would never make it.

Lowie and Tenel Ka dove overboard, hoping for a safe place to land.

Behind them, the TIE bomber crashed into the Shadow Academy's battle platform and exploded in an instant. Its entire cargo of remaining explosives detonated along with the engines, blasting a hole entirely through the immense vessel.

Armored plates flew like metallic snowflakes in all directions. A gout of fire and smoke blasted into the sky, and the cumbersome battle platform plummeted, choking and rumbling.

The mass of unrecognizable wreckage exploded several more times as it plunged into the river. . . .

16

LASER BLASTS FROM the pursuing TIE fighters spanged against Jaina's stolen Imperial ship. One blast sizzled off a corner of the hexagonal power array, sending up a shower of sparks.

She fought to maintain control as her ship began to spin. She lost power, but still her ship flashed onward, propelled by its stealth drive. The silent engines had been made for covert action—not for all-out speed. Behind her, the furious TIE fighters closed the distance.

Jaina flew a frantic evasive action, up and down, diving toward the jungle treetops and then pulling up, hoping the Imperial pilots would make a mistake—slam into a tree branch or collide with each other or something.

No such luck.

The three pursuers had reached point-blank firing range, and Jaina had to take one last gamble. Using the mental speed given to her by Jedi training, she spun the TIE fighter about like a rotating ball, up and over, so that an instant later she headed not away from them, but straight *toward* them! The distance closed in a flash. Jaina had time for only a single shot.

And she didn't waste it.

The blast from her laser cannon ripped open the bottom of one of the TIE fighters, severing its controls, breaking the cockpit's airtight seal. The pilot fell through the hole and tumbled toward the jungle.

Jaina roared between the other two TIE fighters, heading as fast as she could in the opposite direction. They wheeled about, taking longer to complete a three-hundred-sixty-degree turn in the air, but within moments they were following again in hot pursuit.

Jaina flicked her gaze across the control panels, searching for anything that might help her, some secret weapon this TIE fighter might have. She doubted she would find anything that her pursuers couldn't counter.

Then her eyes fixed on a small button: TWIN ION ENGINE SHUNT. Suddenly she realized this would add the TIE fighter's normal engines back to the low-powered stealth drive her fighter had been using.

Without hesitation, she toggled the button off, deactivating the shunt—and with a screech of power, her TIE fighter leaped forward. The roar of acceleration slammed her back against the seat, jolting her lips into a grimace. The ship pulled forward faster than anything Jaina had ever felt.

If she could gain enough of a lead and head straight up into orbit, if she could swing around the jungle moon out of visual range, she could cut her engines for a while and drift out into black space. The stealth coating on this ship's armor would be an enormous advantage. If she could just get out of sight, she could make her ship invisible . . . and she would be safe.

Making use of the ship's acceleration, working with her hands against the increased gravity from the thundering flight, Jaina tilted upward on a straight-line course through the atmosphere, up into space.

The remaining pair of Imperial fighters streaked after her. She didn't know if her acceleration allowed her to fly much faster than the TIE's normal power, but she knew she had to gain distance and use all of her wits.

The atmosphere thinned to a deeper purple, and then the midnight blue of space. To her dismay, she saw that the remaining TIE fighters had closed the distance again, not as much as before, but to within visual range. Her plan wouldn't work—she could never dodge them and disappear against the silent blackness. Her stealth armor would be useless now.

She wondered if she should fight them head-on again. There was a chance that she could take out both Imperial ships before they shot her down . . . but she doubted it.

She was done for.

Just at that moment of despair, Jaina saw a glimmering in the blackness as new ships emerged from hyperspace—reinforcements! New Republic warships! Her heart leaped. It was a small fleet, but well armed, ready to take on the Shadow Academy. Her brother's distress signal must have gotten through.

With a whoop of delight, Jaina adjusted course and shot like a projectile straight toward the fleet of Corellian gunships and corvettes, the quickest bunch the New Republic had been able to muster for the Jedi academy.

Her stolen TIE fighter vibrated as she pushed the acceleration far beyond the red lines. She was still losing power from her damaged side array. "Come on, come on," Jaina said, biting her lip. The ship had to last only a few moments longer. Just a few moments.

The front Corellian corvette loomed closer and closer. But the enemy TIE fighters clung right behind her, still shooting.

Jaina spun and dodged until finally she came into range of the New Republic ships. They began firing huge turbolaser bolts that streaked so close to her ship that the crackling beams dazzled her eyes.

It took Jaina a moment to realize that the gunships were shooting at *her*!

She quickly understood her folly. Here she was in an Imperial ship diving toward the fleet with two more TIE fighters right behind her, laser cannons blasting. It must have looked like all three craft were on some sort of a suicide run.

She grabbed the comm system, toggled it to an open channel, and broadcast at full power. "New Republic fleet—don't shoot, don't shoot! This is Jaina Solo. I've commandeered an Imperial fighter."

More ships appeared at the side, heavily armed hodgepodge vessels bearing the insignia of GemDiver Station, Lando Calrissian's Corusca-gem processing facility that orbited the gas giant Yavin.

"Jaina Solo?" Lando's voice came over the comm system. "Little lady, what are you doing out here?"

"Turning into space dust, if you guys don't take care of the two TIE fighters on my tail!"

Admiral Ackbar's voice broke in. "We're targeting now," he said. "Do not fear, Jaina Solo."

"I'm in the *front* one," she reminded him nervously. "Don't hit the wrong TIE fighter! Well, what are you waiting for?"

A flurry of turbolaser strikes lanced out around Jaina in a pattern so dense that space became a web of deadly weapons fire. Dozens of bolts shot from the Corellian gunships and Lando Calrissian's private fleet. Within moments the two TIE fighters were vaporized, and Jaina let out a long sigh of relief.

Sending a signal from the front Corellian corvette, Admiral Ackbar guided her to the forward docking bay. "Please come aboard, Jaina Solo," he said. "We will offer you sanctuary for the time being while we combat the Shadow Academy. We believe that is the best way to protect personnel on the surface."

"Sounds good to me," Jaina said. "But as soon as it's clear, I want to get back down to fight next to my brother and friends."

"If we do our job well," Ackbar said, "there won't be much of a fight left."

After docking, Jaina climbed out of the stolen TIE fighter, perspiring heavily and glad to be free of the Imperial ship. She no longer felt a great desire to fly one of the craft. Her first experience had been exciting, but not necessarily one she wanted to repeat.

Greeting some of the New Republic soldiers, Jaina quickly ran her fingers through her long, straight brown hair and then rushed to a turbolift. When she arrived on the bridge, she stood beside Admiral Ackbar and watched the fleet attack the ominous spiked station.

New Republic warships pummeled the Dark Jedi training center in orbit over

Yavin 4. The Shadow Academy's powerful shields remained up, but the constant bombardment took its toll.

Lando Calrissian's ships swooped closer, adding their weapons fire. Under the combined onslaught, the Shadow Academy would surely be destroyed before long, Jaina thought.

Ackbar sent out a transmission. "Shadow Academy, prepare to surrender and be boarded."

Jaina didn't have time to relax, though. The Shadow Academy did not bother to answer, and one of the tactical officers suddenly shouted, "Admiral Ackbar, we're detecting a surge in hyperspace, off to starboard. It appears that an entire—"

As Jaina watched the viewscreen, a group of terrifying Imperial ships appeared, Star Destroyers that looked as if they had been hastily assembled and modified. Hasty or not, their weaponry was new and lethal.

"Where did *that* fleet come from?" Lando squawked over the comm channel.

Ship after Imperial ship arrived, an entire, fully armed fighting force that owed allegiance to the Second Imperium. Before even orienting themselves, the Imperial ships opened fire on the New Republic fleet.

"Shields up!" Admiral Ackbar ordered. He turned to Jaina, his round, fishy eyes swiveling in alarm. "It appears that we may experience some difficulty after all," he said.

17

LUKE SKYWALKER ARRIVED across the river at the Massassi ruin known as the Temple of the Blue Leaf Cluster, a tower of crumbling stone blocks. He came alone, hoping to negotiate but ready to fight.

This was the site Brakiss had chosen for their meeting, their confrontation . . . their *duel*, if it came to that.

Luke listened to the jungle noises: the chatter of creatures in the underbrush, birds in the vines overhead—and explosions from Imperial fighters in the sky. He hated to be here by himself when he could be beside his students, fighting with them to defeat the forces of the dark side.

But Luke had a greater calling, a more important one —to stop the leader of these Dark Jedi, a man who had once been Luke's own student.

Branches parted in a thicket beside the

carved pillars of stone. A man stepped out, moving as if he were made of flowing quicksilver, a confident liquid shadow. His perfectly formed, sculpture-handsome face smiled. "So, Luke Skywalker, once my Jedi Master—you have come to surrender to me, I hope? To bow to my superior abilities?"

Luke did not return the smile. "I came to speak with you, as you requested."

"I'm afraid speaking won't be enough," Brakiss said. "You see my Shadow Academy overhead? The battle fleet of the Second Imperium has just arrived. You have no hope of victory, despite your meager reinforcements. Join us now and stop all this bloodshed. I know the power you could wield, Skywalker, if you ever let yourself touch the powers you have neglected to learn."

Luke shook his head. "Save it, Brakiss. Your words and your dark-side temptations have no effect on me," he said. "You were once *my* student. You saw the light side, saw its capabilities for good—and yet you ran from it like a coward. But it's not too late. Come with me now. Together we can explore what remains of the brightness in your heart."

"There is no brightness in my heart," Brakiss said. "I did not come here to banter with you. If you won't be sensible and surrender, then I must defeat you and take the rest of your Jedi academy by force." He withdrew a lightsaber from the silvery sleeve of his robe. Long spikes like claws surrounded the energy blade that extended as he pushed the power button. Brakiss heaved a quick sigh. "This seems like such a waste of effort."

"I don't want to fight you," Luke said.

Brakiss shrugged. "As you wish. Then I'll cut you down where you stand. That makes it easier on me." He stepped forward and swung his blade.

Luke's reflexes kicked in at the last instant, and he leaped back, using a touch of the Force to add power to his spring. He landed with legs spread, crouching, and pulled his own lightsaber from the belt at his waist. "I will defend myself, Brakiss," he said, "but there is so much you could learn here at the Jedi academy."

Brakiss laughed mockingly. "And who's going to teach me—you? I no longer recognize you as a Master, Luke Skywalker. There is so much more that you yourself don't know. You think *I'm* weak because I left here before I completed my training? Who are you to talk? You were only partially trained yourself. A short time with Obi-Wan Kenobi before Darth

Vader killed him, then a brief time with Master Yoda before you left him . . . you even came close to true greatness when you went to serve the resurrected Emperor—and you backed away. You've never completed *anything*."

"I don't deny it," Luke said, holding his lightsaber in a defensive position. Their blades clashed with a sizzling sound. Brakiss's lips drew back in a grimace as he lunged again, but Luke parried his attack.

"You taught that becoming a Jedi is a voyage of self-discovery," Brakiss said. "I have continued that self-discovery since I left here. I abandoned your teachings, but I found more, *much more*. My self-discovery has been vastly greater than your own, Luke Skywalker, because you have locked many important doors to yourself." He raised his eyebrows and his eyes glinted a challenge. "*I* have looked behind those doors."

"A person who willingly steps into mortal danger is not brave," Luke said, "but foolish."

"Then you are a fool," Brakiss said. He swept his lightsaber low, intending to slice off Luke's legs at the knees—but Luke lowered his blade in turn and went on the offensive, clashing, striking, driving his opponent back. The Dark Jedi's silvery robes fluttered around him like nightwings.

"You can't win, Brakiss," Luke said.

"Watch me," the Master of the Shadow Academy said. He attacked with greater fury, opening himself up to anger so that his viciousness grew as he struck again and again.

But Luke maintained his quiet center as he defended himself. "Feel the calm, Brakiss," he said. "Let gentleness flow through you . . . peaceful, soothing."

Brakiss merely laughed. His perfect blond hair was tangled and plastered to his head with perspiration. "Skywalker, how many times will you try to turn me? Even after I fled your teachings, you pursued me. Don't you know when you have lost?"

Luke said, "I remember our confrontation at that droid manufacturing facility on Telti. You could have joined me then—you still can now."

Brakiss dismissed that with a snort. "Those events meant nothing to me, a diversion until I found my true calling—forming the Shadow Academy."

"Maybe you need to look for a truer calling," Luke said. He slashed sideways to deflect Brakiss's lightsaber again.

Now Brakiss took a different tack, whirling around. Instead of striking at Luke, he slashed one of the tall temple pillars, a cylinder of marble etched with ancient Sith symbols and Massassi writings. Sparks flew from the blow, and the lightsaber sheared the column completely through. Gravity, clinging vines, and the overhanging stone made it unstable.

Luke dove out of the way as the pillar split in two. The front lintel of the Temple of the Blue Leaf Cluster tumbled down. Stones and branches crashed from side to side, broken stone flew in all directions— but Luke danced out of the way, avoiding injury.

"You seem quite light on your feet, Skywalker," Brakiss said.

"You seem quite destructive to ancient structures," Luke said. He scrambled over the new rubble, coughed in the settling dust, then clashed again with Brakiss. "Perhaps you should check on how your Dark Jedi are doing. My students have been defeating them quite consistently."

He heard the battle continuing in the jungles and longed to get back to his trainees. The meeting with his former student had been no more than a distraction; it was leading nowhere. "This has gone on long enough, Brakiss. You may either surrender or I'll defeat you directly, because I have work to do. I need to get back to defending my Jedi academy."

Brakiss showed the faintest glimmer of uncertainty in his normally calm and peaceful eyes when Luke drove in, this time intending to win. Luke struck again with the lightsaber, always maintaining his focus and drive, not letting anger take control, doing only what he wished to do.

The Master of the Shadow Academy defended himself, and Luke saw his chance to strike. He altered his aim just slightly, not striking the energy blade itself. He could have swung lower to take off the hand of his former student, much as Darth Vader had cut off Luke's own hand—but Luke didn't want to maim Brakiss in such a way. He needed only to ruin his weapon.

His lightsaber struck across the top of Brakiss's handle, just below the terminus of the energy beam and above the knuckles of the grip. The top two centimeters of the spiked-claw end of Brakiss's lightsaber sprayed off, sheared away in a smoking, molten mass.

Brakiss shrieked and dropped his sparkling lightsaber to the ground, where it lay useless, smoldering, no longer a weapon, simply a hunk of components . . . none of which worked.

The Master of the Shadow Academy held up his hands and staggered back. "Don't kill me, Skywalker! Please don't kill me!"

The terror on Brakiss's face seemed all out of proportion to the threat. Surely the shadow Jedi knew that Luke Skywalker was not the type to strike down an unarmed enemy in cold blood. Brakiss clutched at his silvery robe, fumbling with the fastenings.

Luke strode toward him, lightsaber extended. "You are my captive now, Brakiss. It's time for us to end this battle. Order your Dark Jedi to surrender."

Brakiss let his robes fall away, revealing a jumpsuit and repulsorpack. "No. I have other business to attend to," he said, and ignited the repulsorjets.

As Luke stared in astonishment, Brakiss rocketed skyward, flying high out of reach. The Dark Jedi instructor must have landed his ship somewhere nearby, Luke realized, and he would no doubt head directly back to the Shadow Academy.

In dismay, Luke watched his fallen student escape once more—defeated, but still capable of causing further damage.

The pain of loss flooded Luke's mind, as fresh as on the day Brakiss first fled the Jedi academy. "Brakiss, I've failed to save you again," he groaned.

The other man dwindled to a small point in the sky and disappeared.

18

IN SPACE, THE Second Imperium fleet fired their weapons.

Ackbar shouted, "All personnel, battle stations!" The Calamarian admiral gestured with his flippered hands. "Shields up! Prepare to return fire!"

The two front-most modified Star Destroyers lunged forward, their turbolaser batteries blazing. Brilliant green streaks sliced out, zeroing in on Ackbar's flagship.

Jaina stood beside the Calamarian admiral and squeezed her eyes shut as the blinding flashes shattered against their forward shields. "The Second Imperium must have been building their fleet in secret," she said. "Those ships look like the construction was rushed."

"But they are still deadly," Ackbar said, nodding solemnly. "Now I know why they stole those hyperdrive cores and turbolaser batteries when they attacked the *Adamant*."

He turned to his communications systems, bellowing orders in his gravelly voice. "Shift target from the Shadow Academy. That training station is a lesser threat than the new battleships. Target the Imperial Star Destroyers."

The weapons officers working at their command stations called out in alarm and dismay, "Sir, our targeting locks won't match! Those ships are broadcasting friendly ID signals. We are unable to fire."

"What?" Ackbar said. "But we can *see* the Star Destroyers."

"I know, Admiral," the tactical officer shouted. "But our computers won't fire— they think those are New Republic ships. It's built into the programming."

Suddenly understanding, Jaina exclaimed, "They stole guidance and tactical computer systems during their raid on Kashyyyk! The Imperials must have installed them in their own ships just to confuse our weapons computers. We'll have to change our targeting locks, or else we won't be able to fire. The 'Identify Friend or Foe' fail-safe systems will prevent it."

Lando Calrissian had been listening on the open channel; his voice now boomed over the comm. "Since my ships from GemDiver Station use different computers, I guess the first round is up to us."

Lando's hodgepodge group of independent ships swept in on the Star Destroyers from all sides, firing a barrage of proton torpedoes at key points to dilute the overall shield strength.

"A little trick I picked up," Lando explained over the comm unit as Jaina stood beside Ackbar watching. "This whole thing reminds me of the battle of Tanaab." Then he gave a whoop of triumph as another volley of torpedoes detonated at once, two of them penetrating the shields and leaving a white-hot chain of flames along the side of one Star Destroyer. Lando's ships kept firing and firing, but now the Imperials began targeting the smaller craft, leaving Ackbar's vessels alone.

"Admiral," Jaina said, "if the Second Imperium is so clever that they can use our own computer systems to trick us, can't we turn the tables—use *our* computers against *them*?"

Ackbar turned his enormous round eyes on her. "What do you have in mind, Jaina Solo?"

She bit her lower lip, then drew a deep breath. The idea was crazy, but . . . "You're the supreme commander of the entire New Republic fleet. Isn't it programmed into the computers that they must accept some sort of override signal from you in cases of extreme emergency—like this one?"

Ackbar stared at her, his mouth gaping as if he needed a drink of water or a long breath of moist air. "By the Force, you're right, Jaina!"

"Well, what are we waiting for?" she said, rubbing her hands together. "Let's get reprogramming."

After destroying his own student Norys to rescue Jacen Solo, Qorl's insides felt deadened, as if the rest of his body had turned into a droid . . . just like his mechanical left arm.

After all his years of training and loyalty, he had betrayed the Second Imperium. Betrayed! He had allowed his heart to decide, rather than following blind obedience and cold ambition.

But young Jacen had been kind to him, had helped rescue him, had shown him warmth and friendship, though Qorl knew he had done nothing to deserve it. . . .

He had taken the twins prisoner, threatened their lives, forced them to repair his crashed TIE fighter so he could return to the Empire. Since then he had made small, secret gestures to repay them, such as when he'd cautiously helped them to escape the Shadow Academy. But killing his own student to protect them . . .

Qorl had committed a grave mistake by making decisions on his own. He should have known better. It wasn't his place to make decisions. He was a TIE pilot, a soldier of the Second Imperium. He helped instruct other pilots and stormtroopers. His allegiance was to the Emperor and his government. Soldiers didn't have the luxury of making up their own minds about which orders to follow and which ones to ignore.

His mind in turmoil, he took his TIE fighter up toward orbit. Most of his squadron had fallen out of formation, attacked or destroyed by unknown defenses on Yavin 4. He should return and report to his superiors. He would have to decide whether to surrender or confess what he had done . . . and face Lord Brakiss's retribution.

Qorl's jaw clenched. *Surrender is betrayal.* How could he be willing to do this? His ship's engines howled as he tore free of the atmosphere and headed straight toward the looming Shadow Academy station.

He saw with astonishment that he had stumbled into the middle of an enormous space battle.

New Republic warships had appeared unexpectedly, firing and firing upon the Shadow Academy. But then came the newly arrived fleet of Second Imperium ships, cobbled-together Star Destroyers, Imperial battle cruisers assembled from leftover pieces in reclaimed shipyards. The new fleet used the computer systems, hyperdrives, and turbolaser batteries that Qorl himself had helped to acquire.

But seeing the Second Imperium's ships filled him with a sense of dismay. The new fleet lacked the grandeur and impressive presence of the original Imperial armada. Qorl had flown on the Death Star, served as part of Grand Moff Tarkin's Imperial Starfleet.

This new fighting force looked somewhat . . . desperate—as if people whose dreams stretched far beyond their resources had leaped into the fray.

Qorl saw the Second Imperium ships pounding the Rebel rescue fleet—but as he watched, the tide turned and clusters of nondescript ships attacked the Star Destroyers.

Then the Star Destroyers' defensive shields

suddenly and inexplicably went down, as if their own computers had switched them off. As if they had agreed to surrender!

Rebel battle cruisers fired into the opening at full strength, ripping great gashes in the hulls of the new Star Destroyers. What was going on? Why didn't his comrades reestablish their shields?

As Qorl flew toward them, frantic to do something to help with the fight, fresh TIE fighters streamed out of the Star Destroyers and began to pound the Rebel ships, though they seemed no more than tiny gnats against Ackbar's great fleet.

Qorl suddenly saw his chance to redeem himself. He had already been a traitor to his rescuers and friends and to the Second Imperium. No matter which choice he made, he would be cursed—he would never be able to live with either betrayal.

At the moment, though, Qorl could join the fight on the side of the Second Imperium and cause whatever damage he could . . . perhaps even die fighting. He was a TIE pilot. He had trained for this. Long ago, he had flown from the Death Star on a similar mission—and now he would make everything right again.

Qorl powered up his laser cannons, weapons that had last been fired against Norys's ship to stop the bully's murderous frenzy. Qorl could now use the weapons against his assigned targets: the Rebel Alliance.

His TIE fighter stormed into the fray from out of nowhere, firing on one of the Corellian gunships, leaving black scorch marks as he strafed along its side. Other TIE fighters joined him, flying in a barely recognizable attack pattern. These fleet members were obviously untrained, having spent very little time even in simulators. But the chaos served the new pilots well as the ships flew around each other, blasting and pummeling with no set goal but to cause damage.

The Rebel fleet responded with heavy turbolaser fire, lancing out in all directions. With a blinding glare, one of the Star Destroyers blew up, its command turret in flames. Another Star Destroyer went reeling, its defenses down; it turned in an attempt to limp away. The Rebel fleet pursued, all weapons blazing.

The Second Imperium was losing. *Losing!*

Qorl shot after the fleeing ships. Some of the TIE fighters sped off into space . . . though Qorl had no idea where they intended to go. Their flagships were destroyed and the

Shadow Academy was under fire. Did they intend to give up?

"Surrender is betrayal," he muttered to himself—and flew directly into the Rebel flagship's line of fire.

Turbolaser bolts shot past, but Qorl dove forward, firing his insignificant laser cannons and diving down the gullet of the beast. He would never give up. This would be his final flash of glory.

The Rebels improved their aim—and the cross fire struck him. Qorl closed his eyes behind his TIE helmet, expecting to vanish in a bright puff of flame, a candle burning for his Emperor.

But the energy weapons had only managed to clip one of his engines and damage part of his power array.

Qorl's TIE fighter spun out of control, away from the battle fleet. Even in his crash restraints, he was thrown from side to side inside his tiny cockpit. Qorl held on, expecting his ship to explode at any moment . . . all the while careening farther and farther away from the continuing space battle.

Still spinning, he saw that gravity had caught him. He was crashing again, plummeting toward the jungle moon of Yavin. . . .

19

BRAKISS RACED HIS high-speed, one-person shuttle away from Yavin 4 and streaked back toward his precious Shadow Academy. He punched the coded controls that would automatically open the launch-bay doors and provide him clear passage back into the safety of the Imperial training station.

The space battle did not concern him. It was just one other event that had gone wrong today.

His heart still pounded from his lightsaber battle with Skywalker down at the temple ruins. His thoughts spun, filled with the resonating words of his former Master. Anger and despair swirled like an uncontrollable storm through his mind, through his emotions.

Every method he knew failed to bring his thoughts back to the cold, quiet levels he required to draw on his fullest powers.

Brakiss even attempted to use some of the hated calming techniques Skywalker had shown him back in his incognito student days—but nothing worked.

Everything was crumbling. His grandiose plans, his carefully trained Dark Jedi, the troops of the Second Imperium—it all faltered here on the verge of what should have been his greatest triumph, the hammer blow that would shake the galaxy. The destruction of the Jedi academy should have been a simple victory.

The Emperor would destroy Brakiss for this failure, but for now he could think only that the Emperor himself remained their last hope. Their only hope. Brakiss would accept his punishment later; for now he needed to do everything in his power to bring about a victory.

He brought his shuttle to dock in the nearly empty bay of the Shadow Academy, where not long ago rows of TIE fighters and TIE bombers had prepared for battle. Tamith Kai had launched her armored battle platform, riding down from orbit with her stormtroopers and Zekk's squad of dark warriors. They had been proud, confident, sure of crushing the light-side Jedi. . . .

Brakiss climbed stiffly out of his shuttle,

straightening his silvery robes, trying unsuccessfully to regain his dignity. Not wanting to be without a Jedi blade, he armed himself from a weapons alcove in the wall with another of the mass-produced lightsabers.

But *how* could he defend himself? He had seen Tamith Kai's battle platform plunge into the river, a flaming hulk of molten slag. Zekk's Dark Jedi had been routed, the TIE fighter squadrons mostly destroyed—and now Brakiss watched the Second Imperium's powerful new fleet being trounced by Rebel battleships that had appeared out of nowhere and had somehow deactivated the Imperial shields!

Brakiss strode out of the docking bay into the near-deserted Shadow Academy. All capable troops had been sent to the surface. Only a few command teams remained here to keep the Imperial station secure.

The sterile corridors should have been hosting a victory celebration, but instead the place seemed like a tomb, an abandoned derelict. The Emperor *must* find some way to save them, Brakiss told himself, to turn the tide of battle so that the Second Imperium could rule the galaxy after all.

Palpatine had cheated death not once, but

twice. After he had perished the first time aboard the second Death Star during the battle of Endor, he had managed to resurrect himself, using hidden clones to prolong his life. And though all those clones had presumably been destroyed, thirteen years later the Emperor was once again back from the dead—without an explanation this time.

Any man who accomplished such feats could surely manage to wrest victory away from a hodgepodge gang of Rebels and criminals, couldn't he?

Holding his head up, trying to summon Imperial pride and hope, Brakiss marched down the steel-plated corridors toward the isolated section of the station. He had to see the Emperor, and he would not be turned away. The fate of the entire war hung on the next few moments!

Outside the sealed doorways stood two of the four scarlet-clad Imperial guards. They wore sinister, projectile-shaped helmets with only a narrow black slit through which they could see. The two guards stiffened, crossing their force pikes to deny him entry. Brakiss strode forward without hesitating. "Move aside," he said. "I must speak with the Emperor."

"He has requested not to be disturbed," said one of the guards.

"*Disturbed?*" Brakiss said, appalled to hear the words. "Our fleet is going down in defeat; our Dark Jedi are being captured. Our TIE fighters are being shot down. Tamith Kai is dead. The Emperor should *already* be disturbed. Move aside. I must speak with him."

"The Emperor speaks with no one." They moved one step forward, holding out their weapons.

Brakiss felt fresh anger boiling within. It gave him strength. The power flowing in his veins tapped directly into the dark side of the Force. He could see why the Nightsister Tamith Kai had found the experience so exhilarating that she kept herself in a constant state of pent-up fury.

Brakiss had no patience for these meddling scarlet-clad obstacles. They were traitors to the Second Imperium—and he responded, letting the Force flow from deep within him.

His lightsaber dropped out of his billowing sleeve and fell firmly into his hand. His finger depressed the power button. A long rippling blade extended out, but Brakiss did not use it as a threat. He had grown tired of threats, of word games and diversions that prevented progress. He unleashed his anger.

"I have had enough of this!" He struck wildly from side to side. His anger narrowed his vision to a tunnel of black static that surrounded his two targets as they scrambled to use their force pikes against him. But Brakiss was a powerful Jedi. He knew the ways of the dark side, and the red Imperial guards had no chance against him.

In less than a second, Brakiss had struck both of them down.

He activated the sealed door mechanism. The security pass codes argued with him, so he used the Force to blow out the circuits. With his bare hands he wrenched the stubborn door aside, then strode into the Emperor's private chambers.

"My Emperor, you must help us," he called. The light around him was red and dim, hot. He blinked, finding it difficult to see—but found no one else around. "Emperor Palpatine!" he shouted. "The battle turns against us. The Rebels are defeating our troops. You must do something."

His words echoed back at him, but he heard nothing else: no response, no movement. He pushed on into another room, only to find it filled with a black-walled isolation chamber, its armored door sealed shut, its side panels held in place with heavy burnished rivets. This was the enclosed compartment the red guards had removed from the special Imperial shuttle. Bulky worker droids had lifted the heavy container out of the shuttle's hold and carried it here.

Brakiss knew the Emperor had secluded himself inside the chamber, protected from outside influences. Brakiss had feared that the Emperor's health was failing, that Palpatine needed this special life-support environment just to survive.

But at the moment, Brakiss didn't care. He was tired of having doors shut in front of him. He, the Master of the Shadow Academy, one of the most important members of the Second Imperium, should not be brushed aside like some civil servant.

He pounded on the armored door. "My Emperor, I demand that you see me! You cannot let this defeat continue. You must use your powers to wrest a victory from the hands of our enemies."

He received no answer. His battering noises quickly faded into the thick, blood-colored light that filled the chamber. Brakiss's heart froze into a chunk of ice, like a lost comet from the fringes of a solar system.

If the Emperor had forsaken them, they were lost already. The battle had turned against the Second Imperium—and Brakiss had nothing more to lose.

He switched on his lightsaber again, held the thrumming weapon—and struck. The energy blade sparked and flared as it cut through the thick armor plating—nothing, not even Mandalorian iron or durasteel blast shielding, could resist the onslaught of a Jedi lightsaber.

He sliced through the hinges. Molten metal steamed and ran in silvery rivulets down the side of the door. He chopped again, hacking out an entrance, tearing open the wall like a labor droid dismantling a cargo container. He stepped aside as the thick chunk of armor plate fell to the deck with a deafening clang.

Brakiss stood waiting, frozen with indecision, as the smoke cleared. He held his lightsaber up . . . and finally stepped inside.

He stared in disbelief. He saw no Emperor, no plush living quarters, not even any complicated medical apparatus to keep the old ruler alive.

Instead, he found a sham.

A third red guard sat in a complex control chair surrounded on three sides by computer monitors and controls. Brakiss saw a library display of holographic videoclips taken over the course of the Emperor's career: the rise of Senator Palpatine, the New Order, early attempts to crush the Rebellion . . . recorded speeches, memos, practically every word Palpatine had spoken in public, plus many private messages. Powerful holographic generators assembled the clips, manufacturing lifelike three-dimensional images.

Brakiss stared in horror as it began to make sense to him.

The red guard lurched to his feet, scarlet robes flowing around him. "You may not enter here."

"Where is the Emperor?" Brakiss said, but as he looked around he already knew the answer. "There *is* no Emperor, is there? This has all been a hoax, a pitiful bid for power."

"Yes," the red guard said, "and you have played your part well. The Emperor did indeed die many years ago when his last clone was destroyed, but the Second Imperium needed a leader—and we, four of Palpatine's most loyal Imperial guards, decided to create that leader.

"We had all of the brilliant speeches and recordings the Emperor had made. We had his thoughts, his policies, his records. We knew we could make the Second Imperium work, but no one would have followed *us*. We had to give the people what they wanted, and they wanted their Emperor back—as you did. You were easy to fool, because you *wanted* to be fooled," the red guard said, nodding toward Brakiss.

The Master of the Shadow Academy stepped deeper into the chamber, his lightsaber glowing with deadly, cold fire. "You tricked us," he said, still in the grip of incredulous horror. "You tricked me—*me*! I was one of the Emperor's most dedicated servants, but I served a lie. There was never any chance for the Second Imperium, and now we are being destroyed here because of *you*! Because of poor planning. Because there is no dark heart to the Second Imperium."

Blinded by rage again, Brakiss flowed forward like an avenging angel, his lightsaber held high. The red guard staggered away from his controls, reaching into his scarlet robes to withdraw a weapon—but Brakiss didn't give him the chance.

He cut down the third Imperial guard, who fell smoking and lifeless onto the array of controls that had created the fake Emperor. The illusion had cheated Brakiss, and the Shadow Academy, and all his Dark Jedi . . . everyone who had devoted their lives to recreating the Empire.

"Now the Empire has truly fallen," he said, his voice hoarse and husky, his face haggard. He was no longer calm, like a statue, no longer a well-polished representative of perfection.

Hearing a noise outside the chopped-open door to the isolation chamber, Brakiss turned to see a flash of red—the fourth and final member of the group of charlatans. Brakiss moved slowly, feeling stiffness and pain, utterly discouraged—but he could not let this last one get away. His honor demanded that the deceivers pay. Brakiss rushed after him.

But the red guard had encountered his slaughtered companions outside and knew that Brakiss had seen all the video controls and holographic apparatus in the isolation chamber. The fourth guard, without hesitation, ran back the way he had come.

Brakiss realized with utter certainty that the glorious dream of a reborn Empire had already failed. His Dark Jedi had lost their battle down on Yavin 4. The Imperial fighters were being trounced—but he would *not* let this impostor, this traitor, escape alive. It would be Brakiss's final moment of vengeance.

With purposeful steps, Brakiss charged after the man. The red guard moved with astonishing speed, fleeing the restricted area and dashing down the empty corridors of the Shadow Academy. Brakiss ran, but the red guard knew exactly where he wanted to go. Exactly.

The last surviving Imperial guard reached the docking bay and dashed toward Brakiss's still-waiting high-speed shuttle.

Arriving at the docking bay door, Brakiss shouted, "Stop!" He held his lightsaber high, wishing he could use the Force to make the guard freeze in his tracks, to follow the command—but the charlatan did not hesitate. He dove into the lone shuttle, raised it on its repulsorlifts, and punched the code to release the magnetic atmosphere containment field.

Brakiss simmered with rage. He wondered if he could get to the Shadow Academy's weapons systems and blow the guard to frozen shards in the vacuum of space. But it would be too late for him.

He felt completely alone on the Shadow Academy. An utter failure. Everything he had tried had backfired on him. And this was the final insult: tricked by a . . . *guard*.

Unbidden, a memory came to Brakiss. When the Shadow Academy had been constructed—ostensibly under the guidance of Emperor Palpatine—as a fail-safe mechanism, enormous quantities of linked explosives had been implanted through the station's structure. That way, if Palpatine ever felt threatened by these new and powerful Dark Jedi Knights, he could trigger the detonation and destroy the Shadow Academy, no matter where it was.

Brakiss stood alone in the hangar bay, watching the tiny shuttle streak farther and farther away. It occurred to him that since there *was* no reborn Emperor, then the four red guards themselves must have kept the secret destruct codes.

As the escape ship fled from the Shadow Academy and the Yavin system, the last surviving guard acknowledged to himself that the military forces he left behind would be defeated utterly. With the success of the Rebel counterattack, there would likely be no Imperial survivors of this day's battles.

The guard had to preserve his secret and maintain the illusion that he and his partners had so carefully constructed as a way to restore themselves to power. He could not afford to leave the Shadow Academy intact if he hoped to cover his tracks. With luck, he might find a position among the many criminal elements insidiously working at the fringes of the New Republic.

The red guard sent a brief signal, carefully coded. He transmitted a dreaded phrase, a string of impulses, that he had hoped never to use.

Destruct.

As his tiny shuttle careened into hyperspace, the spiked ring of the Shadow Academy flowered into a fireball, an exploding blossom of flaming gases and debris.

20

AS HE PLODDED ahead, Zekk could barely see two meters in front of himself in the murk of Yavin 4's unfamiliar jungle. Dense underbrush tore at his hair and cape, and his breath came in ragged gasps. His ponytail had come entirely undone. Still Zekk pushed on. Occasionally he glanced back over his shoulder to see if any of Skywalker's Jedi trainees were pursuing him. He sensed no one following, but he couldn't be sure. Who knows? he thought. They might have light-side tricks he had never heard of, ways to keep him from sensing their presence.

He had seen many unexpected things today. Strange things. *Horrible* things. It hardly mattered that the winding path ahead was uncertain and difficult to see: he would have been blind to it anyway. His mind was partially numbed by the sights his eyes had witnessed today. Destruction, terror, failure . . . death.

Zekk's foot slipped on a patch of moldy, damp leaves, and he went down on one knee. Grabbing a low branch, he pulled himself back to his feet, then stood disoriented for a moment.

Which direction had he been heading? He knew he was going *toward* something . . . but he couldn't quite remember what. Finally some unconscious part of him remembered, and he set off again.

Suddenly, just ahead of him, a knee-high rodent sprang from the underbrush, its claws extended. Zekk's Jedi instincts automatically took over.

In one smooth movement Zekk withdrew his lightsaber and threw himself sideways out of the creature's path. His cheek split open as it smashed against the purplish-brown trunk of a Massassi tree; his thumb pressed the lightsaber's ignition stud at the same moment. Before Zekk could even blink or breathe, the blood-red blade sprang forth— and sliced through the rodent in mid-leap. With a shriek that broke off abruptly, the two smoking halves of the creature fell to the forest floor.

It reminded him of how he had killed

Tamith Kai's student Vilas in the zero-gravity arena aboard the Shadow Academy station—not a memory that comforted him.

Blood trickled from the cut on Zekk's cheek, but the pain was too distant, too far away for him to feel. His ability with the Force had protected him just now—after all, he was a Dark Jedi. But what about his companions from the Second Imperium? What of *their* powers? Why had it all gone wrong? For today he had seen his Dark Jedi, one after another, lose their battles or be captured by Skywalker's trainees.

He had a terrible suspicion that only he remained.

Oh, the dark side had had its victories. The commando Orvak had obviously succeeded in destroying the shield generators and had no doubt moved on to the next step in his mission. And there had been other times during the day when Zekk had felt the Shadow Academy trainees achieve surges of victory. But each victory had been short-lived.

Brakiss, Tamith Kai, he, and his companions had all been so certain of a quick, decisive triumph. With their training in the dark side, they should have had no problem,

Zekk told himself. Wasn't that what Brakiss had taught?

A few minutes later, Zekk emerged from the darkness into a broad clearing where the wide river ran sluggishly between the trees. His spirits rising ever so slightly, Zekk walked to the edge of the river and stooped to take a drink.

Despite the green color of the water, his reflection was clear. Sunken emerald eyes shadowed with dark circles gazed back at him from the rippling surface. Only the barest spark of his former confidence still lurked in his expression. Tangles of filthy dark hair framed a face as pale as the moon of his home planet Ennth. Blood still oozed from the wound on his face, contrasting nicely with the purpling bruises that surrounded it. It made him think of Brakiss and his finely chiseled features.

A wail of despair echoed through the young man's head, knocking him to his hands and knees in the mud of the riverbank. In a futile gesture, Zekk pressed his muddy hands over his ears. "Brakiss!" he screamed. "What went wrong?"

Hardly understanding what was happening, Zekk turned his face up toward the sky. For a split second he recognized the spiked ring of the Shadow Academy in low orbit above the jungle moon—

Then, without warning, the space station bloomed into a fireball high above him. Zekk's jaw went slack at the sight. He had not thought it possible to feel any more pain.

But he had been wrong.

Brakiss. The name whispered now in Zekk's mind. He knew that the Master had been aboard the Shadow Academy when it blew up. He could *feel* it. He had felt his teacher's despair—his mind crying out.

The silvery-robed Jedi had taken Zekk in when the young man had had no hope for his future and no purpose. Brakiss had trained Zekk, given him purpose, direction, position, and skills to be proud of. At the Shadow Academy Zekk had *belonged*. He had been its Darkest Knight.

Now what was left for him? All that he had trained for and lived for was gone. Pride, comrades, future . . . all gone. There was no doubt in Zekk's mind that the Second Imperium had been decisively defeated today, and now his mentor—the only man who had ever believed in Zekk—was dead.

No. Not the *only* man who had believed in Zekk. A fresh wave of anguish washed over

Zekk at the thought. Old Peckhum had always believed in him, too. Zekk had promised never to do anything to hurt or disappoint the old spacer. Today, though, he had fought on the side of Peckhum's enemies. Despite all the faults that Zekk acknowledged he had, he had never in his life lied to old Peckhum.

Anger jolted through him—at himself, at having been forced to fight his friend, at having been forced to make such terrible choices. His muscles tightened until the tension inside seemed unbearable. With a cry of anguish he plunged his fingers deep into the mud. It was dark, slippery, treacherous. Yet this was what he had chosen: the darkness.

Today he had stood and watched as his comrades blasted the *Lightning Rod* out of the skies. For all he knew, the only other man who had ever believed in him might also now be dead. Zekk's hands clenched in the ooze and he jerked up fistfuls of mud and smeared it on his face. The mud stung his cut. Now he could feel pain again. But he didn't care. He deserved it.

He had failed them all—Brakiss, the other Dark Jedi warriors, old Peckhum . . . himself. Silent tears dropped unheeded from his eyes as he scooped up more and mud and rubbed it into his hands, his forearms, his neck. Dark mud.

This—*this* was what he had become. Darkness. He had chosen it, immersed himself in it. He was *stained* with it.

There could be no turning back for Zekk anymore. He had made his choices, and he was what he was: a Dark Jedi. That could not change now. Though his comrades were defeated or captured, and Brakiss dead, Zekk would never be able to cleanse himself for as long as he lived—however long that might be.

Not even Jaina and Jacen, if they were still alive, would be able to forgive him. Considering the space battles above, the destruction of the Shadow Academy, the attacks here on the ground, Zekk himself was responsible for a hundred or more deaths today. Maybe even Peckhum's. The twins would know that. They had never believed Zekk's decision to join the Shadow Academy was the right one, had never believed that he could become anything.

But he had made his choice and he had done his best. He had even warned Jaina on Kashyyyk not to return to Yavin 4, hoping to keep her away from the fighting, though he doubted she had listened.

He pushed himself to his feet and caught sight of his reflection again in the slow-moving water. His once-beautiful cape hung in tatters from his shoulders, its scarlet lining shredded. Mud covered his skin. And the sunken emerald eyes were now bleak and hopeless.

But he wasn't finished yet. It might not matter anymore what happened to him, but he still had choices. He would show the twins what he was made of. Turning, he headed along the riverbank toward the Great Temple.

Zekk still had one card left to play.

21

"DOWN THERE," JAINA said, pointing at the jungle clearing that Luke had chosen as a rendezvous point.

From the pilot's seat of his personal shuttle, Lando Calrissian grinned, flashing his beautiful white teeth. "Sure thing, little lady," he said. "I'll take 'er down. Looks like they're waiting for us. The fighting must be done."

As Lando brought the ship in for a landing, Jaina used Jedi techniques to relax, but it did her no good. Her muscles remained as tense as if she were still in the tiny TIE fighter flying for her life. For some reason, she just couldn't loosen up. For the first time, today, she had fought as a Jedi, with other Jedi, against the dark side.

It was what all her training had been about.

When Lando's shuttle touched down, Jaina wasted no time on formalities. She scrambled out of the ship as quickly as she could, ran to her uncle, and threw herself into his arms. "You made it. You're alive!" she said, feeling a surge of relief and jubilation.

"Luke, old buddy!" Lando said. "I came to offer you some help, but it looks like you've got things pretty well under control."

"We could still use your help, Lando," Luke replied. He hugged Jaina back and said soberly, "I'm afraid many of our number were not so lucky."

Realizing that she had no idea how the ground battle had gone, Jaina bit her lip and looked around wildly, hoping to spot Jacen, Lowie, and Tenel Ka.

What she saw shocked her. As far as she could tell, no student from the Jedi academy had escaped unscathed. Several trainees limped. Tionne's right arm hung in a sling and the hair on the right side of her head was singed. Others sported scratches and bruises, as well as more serious injuries.

Jaina stared in surprise when she saw Raynar, his face muddy and his bright clothing torn and covered with filth, moving among the wounded and offering assistance wherever he could. He seemed subdued.

When she noticed the patient Raynar was currently tending, she blanched and dashed over to where Tenel Ka lay, looking feverish and bleeding heavily from a nasty gash just above one gray eye. Another shallower wound ran along her thigh and ended at the knee.

Raynar was already tearing strips of cloth from his relatively clean inner robes. Jaina made a pad of the cloth and pressed it to Tenel Ka's head wound to stanch the flow of blood, while Raynar bandaged the leg cut.

Jaina looked around, still searching for Jacen. Only a few meters away, though she hadn't noticed him before, Lowie lay flat in the grass, moaning quietly and clutching his side.

Around the edges of the clearing, Tionne, Luke, and Lando helped the injured stragglers. There was still no sign of Jacen, though.

"Lowie, are you all right?" Jaina asked.

The Wookiee rumbled something noncommittal and waved a hand, as if to tell her to finish caring for Tenel Ka first.

"Oh, Mistress Jaina! Thank goodness you're here," Em Teedee cried. The little droid's voice sounded strange, and Jaina noticed that the speaker grille was bent. "You have simply no idea what the three of us have been through today. Master Lowbacca and Mistress Tenel Ka were forced to dive from the battle platform in order to avoid being blown up. Which was a good thing, since the battle platform crashed only moments later.

"When we fell to the trees, Master Lowbacca was able to catch himself, but Mistress Tenel Ka struck her head on a branch. She nearly fell all the way to the forest floor, but Master Lowbacca dove after her, caught her arm, and broke their fall by landing stomach-first on a wide limb. Oh, it was bravely done, I assure you, Mistress Jaina. I'm no medical droid, of course, but I'm afraid you'll find that Master Lowbacca has a dislocated shoulder and at least three broken ribs."

Raynar pressed a fresh compress over Tenel Ka's head wound and began winding a bandage around it to hold it in place. "You go ahead," he said, nodding toward Lowie. "I'll finish here."

When two more wounded Jedi students staggered into the clearing, Jaina looked up hopefully, but neither was Jacen. "Have you seen my brother?" she asked Raynar as she went to Lowie's side and knelt to examine his injuries. "He went in the *Lightning Rod* with old Peckhum to call for reinforcements. He should be back by now."

Raynar frowned and shook his head. "Well . . . well . . . I saw the supply shuttle— the *Lightning Rod*. I . . . think one of the TIE fighters hit it."

Jaina gasped. "Did they crash?"

Raynar looked away. "I don't know. The ship seemed to be going down, but . . ." He shrugged uncomfortably. "Anyway, it was hours ago."

Jaina bit her lower lip and closed her eyes, reaching out with the Force, searching for Jacen. "He's not dead," she said at last. "But that's all I can tell. Can't feel old Peckhum—don't have a link with him like I do with Jacen—but my brother's definitely out there somewhere."

A genuine smile broke out on Raynar's face. "Well, good," he said. "That's good."

"That's the last of them, I think," Lando said, striding up and kneeling beside Jaina. "How are you doing, Lowbacca, old buddy? You look like you've seen some hard action."

Lowie gave an *urff* of agreement.

"I think we got everybody who's in the neighborhood now," Lando said.

"We did find one more," Luke said, coming up to join them. He pointed toward the edge of the clearing, where Tionne was tending a treelike Jedi with a broken limb.

Jaina looked up at her uncle. "What about Jacen?"

"He's alive . . . ," Luke said slowly. "We don't know any more than that."

"Yes," said Jaina, "but where is he? Shouldn't we go look for him?"

"We need to get the injured back inside the Great Temple first," Luke said. "If old Peckhum and Jacen managed to get the *Lightning Rod* going, the first place they'd head is the landing field. They wouldn't be able to land in a small clearing like this."

Jaina's spirits brightened. It was true. She looked at Lowie. "Can you walk?" she asked.

Lowie groaned an affirmative reply.

"Master Lowbacca believes himself to be quite capable of perambulation with only minimal assistance," Em Teedee supplied.

"Okay then," Jaina said, "let's get back to the Jedi academy." She was anxious to see her brother again, eager to know that he was all right.

It was close to an hour later when the band of hobbling, limping Jedi trainees finally emerged from the jungle near the Great Temple's landing field. To Jaina's dismay, the flat patch of cleared ground stood empty.

"Don't worry, little lady," Lando said. "I'll help you look for them."

Jaina heaved a sigh and nodded. Even though she knew that Jacen was alive, she had a feeling of foreboding, of impending danger. "All right," Jaina said. "Let's get the wounded inside first. They'll be safe and protected in the temple. We'll have to take them in through the courtyard door, though. The hangar bay's blocked shut."

Crossing the landing field to the flagstone courtyard seemed to take longer than Jaina remembered it, but finally the entrance was only ten meters away. Seeing her goal so close, Jaina smiled and sped up.

Suddenly, a ragged figure lurched out of the shadowy doorway. His face was bloodied and bruised and covered with a thick layer of mud, but Jaina would have recognized him anywhere.

Zekk raised his chin proudly and stood barring the doorway.

"No one goes inside the temple," he said.

22

FACE-TO-FACE WITH HER old friend Zekk again, Jaina could find no words. Her breath refused to move in and out. It seemed to have frozen in her lungs like a chunk of winter. Her heart raced, and her palms grew sweaty.

Zekk didn't move.

Luke came forward to stand beside Jaina. On her other side, still partially supported by her, Lowie voiced a soft growl. And behind her, Jaina suddenly felt the presence of all the remaining Jedi trainees—people who had never met Zekk before today when he had led the attack against the Jedi academy. They saw him only as an enemy, without a glimmer of his being anything else.

Her eyes still fixed on Zekk's mud-covered face, Jaina said, "This is up to me, Uncle Luke. I need to handle this alone."

Luke hesitated for a moment. Jaina knew

that her request was difficult for him. His voice held an undercurrent of warning when he spoke. "This isn't a broken machine that you can tinker with and fix."

"I know," she said softly. "I'm not sure he'll listen to me, but I know he won't listen to anyone else."

"I remember thinking the same thing," Luke said, "when I set out to turn Darth Vader back to the light side. It's a dangerous thing to attempt . . . and success is so rare." He sighed, as if thinking of Brakiss.

Jaina tore her eyes away from Zekk and turned to look at her uncle. "Please let me try," she said. Luke studied her for a long moment and then nodded.

Jaina focused her full attention on Zekk now, shutting out all other distractions as Luke took Lowie away across the courtyard. She drew strength from the Force, but was at a loss as to what to say to the young man.

Where did one start when talking to a Dark Jedi?

Zekk, she reminded herself. This was her friend. She took a step toward him and raised her voice, though only enough so he could hear. "The fighting's over now, Zekk. We just need to get inside to tend our wounded."

Zekk shuddered from an inner chill. He backed up a step and spread his arms across the temple entrance. "No. There'll be a lot more injuries if you don't stop where you are."

Jaina balked at the threat. She would need to try a different tack.

Zekk's eyes darted from side to side, as if he were assessing the strength of the Jedi trainees, with their various wounds, wondering how many he could kill before they took him down.

"Let me be your friend again, Zekk," Jaina said. "I miss being your friend." He flinched as if he had been struck. "Let go of the dark side and come back to the light. Remember the fun we always had together, you and Jacen and I? Remember the time you salvaged that old slicer module and we tapped into the computers at the holographic zoo?"

Zekk nodded warily.

"We reprogrammed all of the animals to sing Corellian tavern songs," she went on. A wistful smile tugged at the corner of her mouth at the memory.

"We got caught," Zekk pointed out quietly. "And the zoo restored the original programming."

"Yes, but so many returning tourists requested it that a few months later the zoo added our singing animals as a separate exhibit." Jaina thought she saw some flicker of acknowledgment in his emerald eyes, but then they became hard as chips of green marble.

"We're not those children anymore, Jaina," he said. "We can't go back to the way it was before. You don't understand that, do you?" His gaze darted around the courtyard and he rubbed one hand across his forehead and eyes, smearing the mud there.

Jaina said, "All right, I *don't* understand. Explain it to me."

Zekk took a deep breath and began to pace in front of the dark doorway, like some wild creature trapped in an invisible cage. "There's no place where I belong anymore, Jaina. The Shadow Academy became my home. It's gone now—completely destroyed. Where can I go? The dark side is a part of me."

"No, Zekk," Jaina said. "You can give it up. Come back to the light."

Zekk laughed, a sound filled with anger and a touch of madness. He clawed at his cheek with one hand and held out his fingers so that she could see the mud there. A wound on his cheek seeped blood, but he seemed not to notice. "The dark side isn't like this mud," he said. "You can't just wear it for a while and then scrape it away— wash it off like some child who has finished playing in the dirt."

Zekk wiped his hand on his tattered cape. "I'm a different person now than the uneducated street kid you knew on Coruscant. I don't belong there anymore. Where *could* I belong? I've been trained as a Dark Jedi." His expression turned bleak. "And now my teacher is dead, too. He taught me and believed in me, gave me skills and a purpose."

"Peckhum always believed in you, too," Jaina said in a gentle voice.

Zekk put a muddy hand to his matted hair, and a wild look came over him. "But he's dead, too—he must be. I saw the *Lightning Rod* go down."

Jaina felt as if she had been rammed in the stomach by a mad herdbeast. The *Lightning Rod* had crashed? Then Jacen could be badly injured.

"I failed my teacher, Brakiss, and he's dead," Zekk said. He gestured as he spoke. "I led the Shadow Academy into battle, and all of my comrades were killed or captured.

And if Peckhum's dead, then that's my fault too." Zekk's eyes looked glassy and feverish; his breathing was fast and shallow.

Jaina set her jaw in stubborn determination. "Well, Zekk, I don't want to see any more people die because of you. Just let me into the temple so we can take care of our wounded."

Zekk stopped pacing and whirled to look at her. "No! Stay back."

Jaina took a step forward. "Zekk, there's nothing left to fight about. What can you possibly hope to gain?"

Zekk shook his head. "You never did listen to my advice. You always thought you knew better." Despite his obvious agitation, Zekk's movements were eerily smooth as he drew his lightsaber from his belt and ignited the glowing red blade with a *snap-hiss*.

Then, in a move so instinctive that a moment later she couldn't even remember it, Jaina found her own lightsaber in her hand, its electric-violet beam humming and pulsating.

A feral grin spread across Zekk's face, almost as if he was glad that it had come to this.

"You see, Jaina," he said, taking a step toward her and twitching his energy blade from side to side, "once you let it in, the dark side is like a disease for which there's no cure." He lunged toward her, and their two blades met in a sizzling struggle of red against violet. "And the only way to remove the disease"—he lunged again and again and Jaina parried—"is to"—*thrust*—"cut"—*thrust*—"it"—*thrust*—"out!"

Jaina spun away and kept a wary eye on Zekk while she circled, waiting for his next move. Out of the corner of her eye she could see Luke watching the battle with calm acceptance.

At that moment Jaina realized that she had been trying to force Zekk to turn to the light side. She had been trying to fix him. But she couldn't. It had to be *his* choice. She drew a deep breath, letting the Force flow through her, and backed away from Zekk.

"I won't fight you anymore, Zekk," she said, switching off her lightsaber and tossing it to the ground. "There's still good in you, but you'll have to decide which direction you want to go—starting now. It's your choice, so make the right one for you."

Surprise and anger and confusion chased each other across Zekk's face. "How do you know I won't kill you?"

From the corner of her eye, Jaina saw

Lowie step forward as if to protect her, but Luke put a restraining hand on the Wookiee's shoulder.

Jaina shrugged. "I *don't* know that. But I won't fight you. Make your choice." Jaina pushed back her straight brown hair and looked directly into Zekk's eyes with calm assurance—not assurance that he wouldn't harm her, but assurance that she had done the right thing.

"Well, what are you waiting for?" she whispered.

With slow deliberation, Zekk raised his glowing red lightsaber over Jaina's head.

23

IMPERIAL COMMANDO ORVAK finally awoke, feeling thickheaded and groggy. He fought away nightmares that were filled with serpent fangs and invisible predators slipping out of cracks in the wall. When he shook his head, a wave of dizziness and nausea pounded through his skull.

Orvak couldn't remember where he was or what he was doing. The stone floor felt hard beneath his sprawled body. He had fallen in an uncomfortable position and apparently slept there for some time. His hand throbbed, and he saw two small wounds there—punctures—before his vision blurred and lost focus again.

He must have taken his gloves off, and his helmet. What had he been doing? Where was he?

He heard no other sounds of combat around the Jedi academy. What could be happening?

Then Orvak remembered creeping into the ancient temple, his important mission for the Second Imperium . . . and the invisible glistening snake that had struck at his hand. For some reason, its venom had knocked him unconscious.

He brought his hand close to his eyes, but clarity of focus continued to evade him. Some kind of poison . . . he had been drugged, but now he was coming out of it. Was he a captive of the Jedi sorcerers?

Orvak heaved himself to a sitting position, and the universe turned in giddy circles around his head. He clutched at the cool, smooth floor for support. He had come here to the temple to plant explosives, to wipe out the great stone pyramid. Then everyone would see the weakness of the Rebellion and its Jedi, and they would make room for the Second Imperium.

But something had gone wrong.

Now he heard something. A clicking. Shaking his head again, he looked in the direction of the strange sound. It came from the timing device across the stone platform from him—

Timing device!

He blinked and finally managed to bring his vision into focus. His eyes burned, but he could see the string of descending numbers on the clock display.

Twelve . . . eleven . . . ten . . .

He launched himself to his feet—but too quickly. Dizziness swept through him again and he fell into black oblivion.

Nine . . . eight . . .

24

THE BUZZING HUM of Zekk's lightsaber filled Jaina's ears as her former friend brought it slowly down toward her neck. "You never understood, Jaina. . . . You can't understand. You've always been so protected. The dark side is like a scar that's on the *in*side."

Zekk's eyes locked with hers. His hand remained steady, and he began speaking in a low voice, his words barely audible. "But these are scars that can't be healed," he went on. "You can try to cover them up"— *hum*; *buzz*—"but they're still there . . . underneath."

A swarm of angry insects buzzed near Jaina's right ear—but it was only the lightsaber, no longer above her head but continuing its excruciatingly slow descent.

Then, as if from a distance, Jaina heard new sounds: a crackle of static, and then a booming voice coming from a comlink.

"This is the *Lightning Rod*, callin' anyone who can hear me. Better clear everyone from the landing field real quick. We're comin' in. Oh, and if you got any of those energy shields back up, you better put 'em down now—we've had more'n our share of problems already today. My arm's broken, so the young Solo kid is flying—but our wings're clipped, and I'm not sure how maneuverable this baby is."

In that moment of delight and surprise, Zekk's lightsaber wavered and lifted away from her. A droning sound caught his attention, and Jaina glanced back over her shoulder to see the *Lightning Rod* coming into view above the treetops, sputtering and wheezing.

"Come on in, *Lightning Rod*," Jaina heard Luke say into his comlink. "You're clear to land."

Zekk stared in amazement to see the battered old ship still intact, then shook his head. He reached out his free hand toward her. "Jaina, I didn't mean to—"

Just then, a concussive boom split the air, obliterating all other sounds. The ground vibrated beneath Jaina's feet, lurching with tremors and shock waves.

"Get down!" Zekk shouted.

She dove toward the courtyard wall and hit the ground, gasping at the jolt of pain that speared through her. She rolled, looking upward to see the gouts of smoke that erupted from a huge explosion inside the Great Temple. The crumbled remnants of massive stones tumbled down its sides in an avalanche.

Zekk ran for cover, too, but the hailstorm of rock moved faster than he could dodge. A large chunk of stone struck him in the head, while other fragments pummeled his body. As Jaina watched the dark-haired young man sink to the ground, it came to her in a flash: he had known.

Zekk had *known* the temple was going to blow up.

And he had saved them all

25

OUT IN THE unexplored jungles of Yavin 4, on the far side of the moon from where Luke Skywalker had established his Jedi academy, the wrecked TIE fighter smoldered after the crash.

The cockpit hatch opened, and Qorl crawled out, coughing and wheezing. With a heave from his human arm, he raised his shoulders, then worked the rest of his body free. His droid arm sparked and sizzled from damage it had received in the crash.

Qorl felt no pain, though. He was still functioning on adrenaline as he hauled himself out of the ship. His legs were numb and stiff, but they still worked. He dropped down from his ruined TIE fighter, then staggered into the protection of the trees just in case the craft exploded.

Alone in the jungle, Qorl watched the TIE fighter smoke until he was confident that none of the engines would go critical. The wrecked ship gradually heaved its last sigh and died.

The damage to his craft was severe: its outer hull had been punctured by iron-hard Massassi tree branches, its two planar energy arrays ripped askew; one had even been broken off.

As he had flown in, pummeled by the Rebel forces, dodging turbolaser bolts until the fatal strike that had caused him to reel out of control, Qorl had seen the Star Destroyers defeated. While wrestling for control of his TIE fighter, he had watched the Shadow Academy explode behind him.

He knew now that all hope for the Second Imperium was gone. The Emperor himself had been aboard the Shadow Academy, as had Lord Brakiss. The remaining Dark Jedi fighters on the surface would no doubt be rounded up and taken to Rebel prisons.

Qorl had much to regret. Rather than let one of the Solo twins die, he had made the choice to sacrifice his twisted student Norys. That had been a betrayal, and he was ashamed of it. Surrender was also betrayal. . . .

But Qorl had never surrendered.

He found himself stranded in the jungle again. His ship was beyond repair. The

Second Imperium was defeated. Qorl had no place to go, no orders to follow . . . no reason to do anything other than search for a new place to live.

Perhaps it was best this way.

He could make a nice home for himself here. He knew this jungle, the fruits that were good to eat, which animals were easiest to hunt. Qorl realized that, despite the glory of returning to the Second Imperium and fighting once more for his Emperor, he had enjoyed those years of solitude, the quiet peace of living alone in the jungle.

In fact, he decided that this fate was not so bad, after all.

Qorl trudged off into the jungle to search out a new home. This time, he intended to spend the rest of his life there.

26

THE MORNING AFTER the great battle on Yavin 4 dawned cool and clear. Within hours, the bright sunlight dispensed with the lingering tatters of lacy mist that clung to the rubble-strewn base of the Great Temple and to the trees around it. Overhead, the giant orange planet Yavin filled much of the sky.

Waiting with Lowie and Jacen on the landing field, Jaina marveled at the difference a night's rest and a good meal could make on her perspective. After Luke, Tionne, Lando, and a couple of GemDiver engineers had determined that the lower two levels of the Great Temple were structurally sound, the remaining trainees and staff had made their way back into the pyramid, retrieving an ecstatic Artoo-Detoo, who had been waiting below. Admiral Ackbar's transports had evacuated the most seriously injured students, while those with only minor wounds had been treated and returned to their own chambers in the temple.

Jaina felt fortunate—and a bit guilty— that she had emerged from the battles almost completely unscathed. She had a few cuts and bruises from where stones had hit her after the explosion, but that was all.

Jaina ran an appraising eye over her friend Lowbacca. His shoulder was back in position again, his arm supported by a wide cloth strap, his broken ribs wrapped. The Wookiee normally wore only his webbed belt made of syren plant fibers, so the sling and the thick white bandaging around his midriff seemed oddly out of place.

She heard a warble and bleep behind her, and turned to find Artoo and her uncle Luke coming across the landing field to join them. The Jedi Master's face held a look of serenity and determination, but his eyes showed a glint of humor.

"I think *I* looked even worse than that," Luke said without preamble, "after my encounter with the Wampa ice creature on Hoth."

"Yes, but Lowie's looking a lot better this morning," Jaina agreed.

Luke chuckled. "Actually, I was referring to the Great Temple itself."

Jaina turned to study the ancient Massassi pyramid. The topmost level had collapsed where the detonators had exploded, and part of the sides had slumped downward. The broken, jagged walls of the grand audience chamber could have been mistaken for crenellations atop the battlements of some ancient fortress.

"At first I thought we might have to move the academy to some other temple," Luke said, "but now . . . I'm not sure we need to."

"You mean we could rebuild it?" Jacen asked with a groan. "Great—more practice exercises, lifting rocks, balancing beams . . ."

Artoo-Detoo twittered and beeped, as if excited at the idea. Lowie rumbled thoughtfully, then growled in pain, holding his aching ribs.

"Yes," Luke said. "In one way or another we've all been hurt through our encounters with the dark side. I think rebuilding the Great Temple might be a part of healing each of our wounds."

"Like Zekk," Jaina murmured, feeling her heart contract painfully. "He needs a lot of healing."

"That reminds me, Uncle Luke," Jacen

said, "what will you do with the Dark Jedi trainees we captured?"

"Tionne and I are working with them. We'll do our best to turn them back to the light side, but if it's not possible . . ." He spread his hands. "I'll have to discuss that with Leia, and—"

"Oh, Master Lowbacca, look!" Em Teedee interrupted from his clip at Lowie's waist. Jaina noticed that the tiny droid's speaker grille had been straightened and meticulously polished.

"Hey, they're back," Jacen cried.

Lando's shuttle, with Lowie's battered T-23 in tow, arrowed toward a corner of the landing field well away from the blaster-scarred hulk of the *Lightning Rod*.

Uttering a joyous howl, Lowie gave Em Teedee a grateful pat.

"Well, what are we waiting for?" Jaina asked as the shuttle and the T-23 touched down.

Jaina, Jacen, and Lowie hurried forward. By the time they reached it, the shuttle's landing ramp had extended, and Lando Calrissian strode down it with Tenel Ka on his arm. Lando's cape swirled behind him and he flashed his most charming grin.

"Your friend here is quite a tough young lady," he said approvingly.

"This is a fact," she said, without the slightest trace of humor.

"I could have told you that," Jacen said. "Did you find it?"

Tenel Ka nodded, a satisfied look on her face. She pulled her arm free, plucked something from her belt, and held it out to show Jacen. It was the rancor-tooth lightsaber that she had lost during her clash with Tamith Kai on the battle platform. "It was not as difficult to locate as I had feared," she said. "Perhaps because I knew the rancor whose tooth this was, I was able to sense its location."

Tenel Ka no longer appeared feverish, and Jaina was amused to note that the warrior girl had braided her red-gold hair carefully around her face so that her bandage looked like a primitive warband across her forehead.

"I've invited Tenel Ka to come and visit GemDiver Station, since she missed it last time," Lando said. "We have some good bacta tanks there that'll fix up that cut on her head no time. Lowbacca, looks like you could use a few days in one of our tanks, too."

Lowie barked his acceptance and a thank-you.

"Oh, that would be exceedingly kind of you, Master Calrissian," Em Teedee said. "Master Lowbacca is most anxious to complete his healing and begin repairs on his incapacitated vehicle."

"His little skyhopper ain't the only vehicle that's incapacitated."

Jaina jumped when Peckhum's loud voice boomed out behind her.

"I know just what he means, though. The boy and I can't wait to get started fixing the *Lightning Rod*. But I think Zekk is going to be laid-up here for a while recuperating." Old Peckhum stood by the damaged *Lightning Rod*, one hand on Zekk's shoulder, the other arm heavily bandaged.

Zekk's face was as pale as the dressing that wound around the base of his skull. His eyes seemed curiously empty, his face expressionless. He did not meet Jaina's gaze.

"I think you've got two more candidates for your bacta tank, Lando," Jaina said. "Can Jacen and I go along with them, Uncle Luke?"

Artoo-Detoo twittered.

"Oh, indeed! That's a marvelous idea," Em Teedee said.

"We promise not to get kidnapped this time," Jacen added with a lopsided Solo-style grin.

Luke chuckled. "All right, I think that would be good for all of you. You young Jedi Knights are stronger together. If you have some time away to heal, then you'll come back ready to help us rebuild . . . ready for a new beginning."

"Thanks, Uncle Luke," Jaina said.

"Jacen, my friend," Tenel Ka said. "Perhaps we had better leave soon. We do not want all of the injured students to come away with us and leave Master Skywalker here alone."

Jacen gave Tenel Ka a quizzical look. "What do you mean?" he said. "Why would you worry about that?"

"Because," Tenel Ka said solemnly, "a Jedi *must* have patients."

Jacen blinked at her, uncertainty written on his face. Then a shy grin lit Tenel Ka's face. It was the first time he had seen her smile so broadly.

"I don't believe it . . . ," Jacen began.

Jaina shook her head in wonder. "Sounded to me like she just told a joke."

"This is a fact!" Jacen said.

Lowie chuffed with delight. Jaina giggled.

Soon the entire clearing rang with laughter.

Watch for the continuing STAR WARS adventures of Jacen, Jaina, and their young Jedi friends!

Now that the Second Imperium has been defeated and the Shadow Academy destroyed, the young Jedi Knights are preparing for an all-new series of adventures.

We planned the first six volumes to tell a complete story arc, introducing the Imperial threat, the Dark Jedi training center, and our heroes and villains. Each book was its own adventure, but built upon the overall tale that would bring Luke Skywalker's young Jedi trainees clashing against their evil counterparts from the Shadow Academy.

When we were asked to extend the Young Jedi Knights series, we decided against writing small adventures one book at a time. Instead, we once again plotted an overall storyline, this one covering volumes 7–11. Rather than making another attempt to bring back the grim glory of the Empire, we opted to use different villains.

Bounty hunters.

The next five books in the saga of the Young Jedi Knights pit Jacen, Jaina, Lowbacca, Tenel Ka, and their friend Zekk against a terrible new threat that could well mean the end to all human life in the New Republic. They travel to strange new worlds, meet old friends and make new allies, all the while continuing their development as Jedi Knights—with a little help from a few familiar characters along the way.

The first volume, *Shards of Alderaan*, brings back Han Solo's greatest nemesis, Boba Fett. Hired by a Twi'lek woman, the charismatic leader of a popular non-human political movement called the Diversity Alliance, Fett searches for a deadly bounty. Once the young Jedi Knights learn what is at stake, and when a group of the surliest and most disreputable bounty hunters also decides to go after the prize, it becomes a race against time with the fate of the human species hanging in the balance.

Watch for new Young Jedi Knights adventures in your local bookstores. Join us as the adventure continues with

Shards of Alderaan
Diversity Alliance
Delusions of Grandeur
Jedi Bounty
The Emperor's Plague

May the Force be with you!

—Kevin J. Anderson and Rebecca Moesta

Turn the page for a
special preview of the next book in the
STAR WARS: YOUNG JEDI KNIGHTS series:

SHARDS OF ALDERAAN

Beginning an all-new Young Jedi Knights
adventure!

*Coming in January 1997
from Boulevard Books!*

Space was vast, an infinite pool in all directions . . . whether up and out of the galactic plane, or deeper inward toward the dense Core Systems. The galaxy held countless hiding places: planetars, asteroid fields, star clusters, gas clouds . . . even these empty wastelands without stars.

It would take the best of bounty hunters to find their quarry under such circumstances.

And Boba Fett was the best.

He cruised along in the wilderness between star systems, all sensors alert, scanning for any sign of his prey. He had dropped out of hyperspace in his ship, the *Slave IV*, and searched just long enough to take data—but his sensitive detectors picked up no energy readings, no sign of any ship's passage within half a parsec. Nothing had crossed this empty no-man's land in the past decade.

Grim and persistent, Boba Fett studied readings through the narrow vertical slit in the faceplate of his Mandalorian helmet. He nodded, speaking no word into the flight recorder. His quarry wasn't here. He would have to search elsewhere. The hunt might be long, but no one could elude Boba Fett in the end.

He clutched the *Slave IV*'s modified controls—propulsion systems, navigational computers and acceleration foils that were illegal in many systems. But Fett paid no attention to legalities. Mere laws did not apply to him. He obeyed his own code of ethics and morality: the Bounty Hunter's Creed.

Launching his ship into hyperspace, Fett replayed the holomessage Nolaa Tarkona had sent to him. His assignment for this hunt. Perhaps he might find other clues there. He already knew the message by heart, had listened to it eight times on his journey, but he replayed the message anyway.

Boba Fett carefully observed the female Twi'lek's face: the folds around her pinkish eyes, the greenish cast to her skin, the white teeth sharpened to points like powerful male Twi'leks did. In the recording, Nolaa Tarkona's green-skinned headtails dangled from the back of her skull and curled around her shoulders. Her voice was deep and melodious, not the dry, crisp hiss he might have expected from a surreptitious crime lord. Tarkona led a growing political movement—the Diversity Alliance. Nothing overtly criminal . . . at least not yet.

Boba Fett did not care about her politics or her reasons. That was not a bounty hunter's business. She was his employer, and he had a job to do.

The hologram spoke. "Boba Fett, your fame has spanned decades and crossed the galaxy— now I offer you the greatest assignment of your career." The Twi'lek woman stroked her headtails. Her eyes looked like discs of rose quartz glowing with internal fire.

"Find the man named Bornan Thul, an important trade commissioner from Coruscant. He was a member of the nobility on Alderaan before that planet was destroyed, and he has become a trade negotiator in the New Republic government. Through my own contacts, I sent him to procure a valuable cargo—certain items crucial to the Diversity Alliance. He was to deliver the shipment to me at an important trade conference where I was scheduled to give a speech. But his ship vanished en route—and my cargo disappeared with him. Find Bornan Thul. I *must* have those supplies back."

She leaned forward, and her mouth opened in a smile, showing off her jagged teeth. "When Darth Vader hired you to find Han Solo, the bounty was quite substantial. I will pay you *twice* that if you find Bornan Thul and bring me my cargo. Other bounty hunters will be searching as well—but you are the best, Boba Fett.

You survived the sarlacc. You have prevailed against the odds and overcome obstacles that would have been the death of lesser bounty hunters. I expect results from you."

Inside his cramped cockpit, Boba Fett switched off the holoprojector and swept his gloved hands through the dissolving sparkles of color as the three-dimensional image faded. "And you will have results," he muttered, his voice loud in the oppressively silent ship.

Approaching another solar system in which there were no catalogued planets capable of supporting life, Fett dropped out of hyperspace to continue his search. His navicomputer had a map of all stars throughout the sector where the trade negotiator had vanished. His data banks were crammed with esoteric information and reports, any one of which might give him a clue that would lead to the discovery of his prey.

Bornan Thul had flown alone in his ship, refusing the diplomatic escort to which he was entitled. Secretly checking through New Republic flight records, Fett saw that this was quite an unusual request for the trade negotiator. The former Alderaan noble preferred large escorts and excessive pomp and ceremony. Flying off alone in a supply cruiser seemed highly uncharacteristic for this man.

Fett wondered if Thul had discovered anything unusual about the nature of his cargo or its importance to the Twi'lek political leader's movement. He himself did not know what the cargo was. Nor did he care. He just had to find it and return it to Nolaa Tarkona.

Fett approached the bleak, uninhabited system—a small double star with three frozen gas planets in distant orbits and two rocky inner planets. After a few moments of scanning, his sophisticated sensors detected processed metal, faint lubricants, traces of stardrive fuel, leakage of spin-sealed Tibanna gas—a strong enough reading to indicate a whole ship. The source seemed to be hiding inside the ragged strands of a rocky ring that surrounded the outermost frozen gas planet.

Boba Fett nodded in respect. A good place to hide, and a good system in which to remain hidden. With bright sublight engines, the *Slave IV* homed in on the signal.

Fett had studied the history and family of Bornan Thul, hoping for clues. Understanding his prey was the best way to catch it. Thul had a wife who remained under heavy security on Coruscant . . . and one son, a young man named Raynar, who had been sent to the best schools, teamed up with the most efficient tutors, and now had been enrolled in Skywalker's Jedi academy. Obviously, Bornan Thul doted on him, gave the boy everything he desired, so that Raynar needed to work for noth-

ing in his life. Boba Fett decided that Raynar
might make a good hostage—if it came to that.

But perhaps it would all end here at this
forgotten, out-of-the-way planet. Much of the
metal signal was indistinct, blurred due to
ionization and outgassing from the broken
rocks and ice chunks in the planetary ring.

As Fett approached, he realized the signal
itself was scattered, spread widely apart. Perhaps Thul's ship had crashed into some ring
debris, scattering wreckage in a broad swath.
A low, growling sound came from deep within
his throat. The bounty would be cut in half if
Fett found only the wreckage of Thul's ship.
The Twi'lek woman cared only about the
cargo.

Fett looked out the *Slave IV*'s cockpit win-
dowport as he cruised into the swirling strip of
rocky debris like a racetrack around the blue-
and-white ice world. Following the sensor signal, he pulled up close to several long chunks of
scattered metal: hull plating, blast shields from
a ruined vessel. Unmistakably, wreckage from a
ship. Recent wreckage.

Fett ran a quick analysis and determined
that the hull plating matched the type of
vehicle Thul had been using. He allowed himself a grunt of disappointment. Perhaps everything had been destroyed, leaving only this
debris. But Fett knew there should have been
more mass . . . much more. His sensors had

picked up a signal strong enough to account for an entire ship, and this debris amounted to no more than a hundred kilograms or so. He wondered where the rest could have gone. Maybe some of the cargo remained intact after all.

He reacted with lightning speed as the attacking vessel came around a frozen methane asteroid. Another bounty hunter ship, shaped like a deadly pinwheel star, its laser cannons already taking aim!

Boba Fett sent *Slave IV* into a spin, twirling out of the way of four rapid-fire laser bolts. The other bounty hunter did not continue to shoot his lasers, powering up an ion cannon instead—which was exactly what Fett would have done. An ion cannon blast would neutralize all power systems on his ship, leaving him dead in space, where his enemy could dissect him at will and strip away all of his possessions and weapons.

A bounty hunter, a good bounty hunter, always attempts to make efficient use of resources.

Fett's weapons systems were not engaged. He mentally cursed himself for not preparing while he approached the suspicious debris. This other fighter had been lying in wait for him. Perhaps the other bounty hunter had found the debris himself, or perhaps he had set it there as a lure. Or perhaps the other bounty hunter had already destroyed Bornan Thul's ship.

As Boba Fett zipped and dodged, the attacker came on, clearly holding the upper hand. Fett tried to accelerate, ducking in and around the rocks of the spiraling planetary ring, but he knew that would merely be a delaying tactic. He had no chance of evading pursuit when his attacker was this close.

A message came over his comm system. "Boba Fett, I recognize your ship. This is Moorlu—the bounty hunter who's going to destroy you." The enemy chuckled, a low phlegmy laugh. "I will display your helmet as my trophy!"

"I'm not a trophy yet," Boba Fett muttered. Planning the best way to defeat his overconfident nemesis, he took a gamble.

Boba Fett allowed himself to be hit.

The ion blast rippled against the *Slave IV*'s hull, frying his electrical systems, leaving him dead in space, so that he drifted around the icy planet, apparently helpless.

Apparently.

"Got you, Boba Fett! Now I can take care of you, steal everything you own—and use it to chase down Bornan Thul."

Moorlu, you talk too much, Fett thought, as the comm system shut down.

Dangling in the arms of zero-gravity, without ship's power, he waited as the other bounty hunter's small, pinwheel ship approached like a spider-rat to disassemble its prey.

Moorlu didn't notice the pneumatic launcher mounted at the rear weapons hatch of *Slave IV*.

Boba Fett cranked the launcher by hand, using mechanical systems only. He waited patiently to take his only chance. At least the comm system had shut down, so he didn't have to listen to Moorlu's obnoxious gloating.

When the other bounty hunter's ship came close enough for a ballistic launch, Fett aimed by sight and triggered the release. A torpedo dart filled with concussion explosives flew across space as if spat from a slingshot.

Boba Fett's aim was true.

The high explosives penetrated Moorlu's hull, ripping out the fuel pods beneath the pinwheel engines, setting up a detonation that left Moorlu dead in space. *Literally* dead in space.

Fett despised bounty hunters that were too easy to kill, but he supposed it cleared the playing field of amateurs. . . .